We Are
What We Pretend
to Be

We Are
What We Pretend
to Be

THE FIRST AND LAST WORKS

Kurt Vonnegut

Vanguard Press
A Member of the Perseus Books Group

Published by Vanguard Press
A Member of the Perseus Books Group

Designed by Brent Wilcox
Set in 11.75 point Adobe Caslon Pro

Cataloging-in-Publication data for this book is available
from the Library of Congress.
ISBN 978-1-59315-743-2 (hardcover)
ISBN 978-1-59315-744-9 (e-book)

Vanguard Press books are available at special discounts for
bulk purchases in the U.S. by corporations, institutions, and
other organizations. For more information, please contact the
Special Markets Department at the Perseus Books Group,
2300 Chestnut Street, Suite 200, Philadelphia, PA 19103,
or call (800) 810-4145, ext. 5000, or e-mail
special.markets@perseusbooks.com.

10 9 8 7 6 5 4 3 2 1

Contents

[v]

Foreword

I am not a student of my father's writing, but I am his daughter and would like to share what I know about both *Basic Training* and *If God Were Alive Today*, both of which are somewhat autobiographical. *Basic Training* is a story that was never accepted for publication. *If God Were Alive Today* is the beginning of a novel that was never finished. They were written at the beginning and end, respectively, of my father's writing career, fifty years apart.

I was not even born when my father wrote *Basic Training* in 1950, but over the years I could swear I remember him talking about someone from his childhood called "the General." As I read the story I felt eerily close to my father, as if I were seeing through his sixteen-year-old eyes, and we were in Indiana in the company of his old friends. So I called his childhood friend, Majie Failey, now ninety years old, to see if there was any fact behind this piece of fiction.

Foreword

As I gave Majie the broad strokes of *Basic Training*, I hit black gold and the memories spilled out of her. My father spent many happy summers on Rainbow Farm, just outside Indianapolis. The General in the story was in fact based on my grandfather's cousin, who had been a captain in the Rainbow Division during World War I and ran his family and farm in the military fashion. My father was in love with one of the three Captain's daughters, Mary, who was quite beautiful and his own age. The Captain wouldn't allow his daughters to visit the city, so, even though my father was terrified of the Captain, he would bicycle out to the farm on weekends and do chores just to be near Mary. As the phone call with Majie went on, it became clear that she had become unstuck in time. She talked about a stallion named Ezekiel, remembering him up on his hind legs snorting, almost hitting the rafters of his stall. The red-haired, green-eyed boy was based on Ben Hitz, and inspiration for the guy in the polished boots and military garb had to be Dad's cousin Sonny Mueller. Ben Hitz was my father's best man when he married my mother.

Later in his life, when my father said he wanted to go home, he always meant to his childhood and home in Indianapolis. This story is, in large part, about sixteen-year-old Kurt Vonnegut at his happiest, before the war.

My twenty-year-old daughter was elated to learn that her grandfather was close to thirty when he wrote *Basic Training*. She felt it meant that time was on her side and she had a chance at being a good writer after all. When my children romanticize the writer's life, I remind them that their grandfather worked at his craft for years with little reward. I describe the piles of rejection letters from publishers that wound up as decoupage on waste-baskets in our house.

It took years of work, producing stories like *Basic Training*, while he was holding other jobs and supporting his young family, for my dad to develop his very own, finely tuned voice. Only two years after he wrote *Basic Training*, *Player Piano* was published.

Gil Berman, the main character in *If God Were Alive Today*, was conceived in my father's slightly charred, seventy-eight-year-old brain in the year 2000. A month before my father came to Northampton, Massachusetts, to be near family after being exiled from his brownstone in New York City, the upper story of his house caught fire, and he wound up in a hospital burn unit with complications from smoke inhalation. His wife of twenty-five years told him that he was not welcome back until the damage was repaired.

I had been squawking for years about how my father was abducted from me by fame and fortune back in 1969 when I was fifteen, the year of *Slaughterhouse Five*. Northampton had a lot to offer—grandchildren, nephews and nieces, writers and artists. When it came time for my father's discharge from the rehab facility, two of my brothers drove to rescue and deliver him to the Hotel Northampton and to me. They called me an hour outside of Northampton and announced, "We're delivering your father."

He was miserable upon arrival. He snapped at me a lot. So much so that I left him a note at the Hotel Northampton, along with keys to an apartment within walking distance from the hotel, saying that I was at his disposal, but only if and when he asked. He took the keys when no one was looking and climbed the steep staircase to the waiting apartment, where he hung the very few pieces of clothing he had. His new home came with a computer to write on and a charming and witty landlady who gradually brought out the courtly Kurt Vonnegut; I saw a little color come back to his cheeks.

He could walk to Serio's, our local grocery store, where they even carried Pall Malls. The Tunnel Bar was practically in his backyard, a place so darkened he would not be recognized, and a place where he could smoke and drink. He made friends with all the clerks at the local hardware store, probably because, as a boy in Indianapolis, he had worked at Vonnegut Hardware. The first thing he bought for his new life was a Waring blender. He could walk to my house for dinner if he felt like it. Sometimes he would come by with shopping bags full of candy and soda for his grandchildren, commanding them to "Live it up!"

I brought my father to a performance of Hal Holbrook's Mark Twain at The Calvin Theater not long after he arrived. My father was transfixed. He communicated his agreement with Mr. Twain's words with quiet coughs and sighs. Toward the end of the performance, Mark Twain said something about having deeply disappointed his wife. This elicited from my father a deep groan. We stayed behind to meet Hal Holbrook. I watched as the two Mark Twains spoke to each other with utmost respect, almost reverence.

Another good day was when I watched my dad goose Gloria Steinem on the steps of the Smith College Chapel, where she was about to deliver a sermon to Smithies. Gloria Steinem turned around, completely composed, and said, "Oh, hello Kurt."

My father and I did a lot of walking when he was in Northampton. The talks were always intense, but they were often broken up by his sudden theatrics, such as when he saw a squirrel freeze in the street with a nut in his mouth, and shouted, "Hey, you, squirrel, drop that nut!" We'd double over laughing for an unnatural amount of time and then return to the very serious subject at hand. He was trying to figure out how to resolve his marital problems. He was considering faking his own death as a possible solution.

Though it had been more than thirty years since I had had any extended amount of time with my father, not much had changed. I still worried that he would not answer the door and I might find him dead. Growing up, suicide was always considered a possible and even logical outcome of my father's life. But my father always answered the door, and I usually found him in the act of writing, which included working on the *New York Times* crossword puzzle. Sitting next to him on his purple velvet futon couch, I'd listen to what he was trying to write. As he talked, his long toes would knead the floor, and I could feel heat waves coming off his head as he was working an idea. He appeared to me then as an exquisite alien creature, as if his giant brain and long toes were trying to extract something from another planet. He told me he was failing to connect with anything worthwhile that day, except his main character, Gil Berman, who might have to fake his own death.

Most times I'd find my father in a very receptive mood to my prying questions, like "How many times have you been in love?" His answer was instantaneous, and he held up three long fingers.

I was relieved to hear my mother was one of them. His explanation of the merits and failures of each true love struck me as completely fair. Whether or not my mother really did not love him enough did not matter; he felt that love was lacking, and I believed him. As I was walking out the door with his laundry, I suggested that we go to therapy together. He answered, "There's too much to talk about!" There was nothing unloving in this answer; he was absolutely right. Sometimes the best thing for me was to tell a good joke and tell it well. When I told him about the old man who confessed to a youth with a colorful Mohawk haircut that he had fucked a parrot many years before, and was wondering if the young man might be his son, my father told me that my delivery was elegant.

Once, I brought to my father's attention a story in the *Boston Globe* about a stockbroker who had killed his wife and staked her head to a pole in the front yard for the entire neighborhood to see. The husband explained that he had gone bonkers when the wife overcooked the pasta for supper. My father paused for about three seconds and replied, "Well, we don't know what she did before that."

Though my father was trying to divorce his wife, the phone calls from the brownstone in New York City were incessant. I was present for one such phone call that went on for a very long time. As far as I could tell, it involved a broken appliance that my father, being the man of the house, should fix somehow. Finally, my father yelled, "Call General Electric for Christ's sake!" Then he yanked the phone line out of the wall.

After almost a year in Northampton, he went back to his

brownstone in New York City, knowing full well he was walking back into a burning house, but it was familiar.

Gil Berman was conceived and born out of the toxic circumstances of my father's life at that time. So, of course, Gil Berman and the story are quite ill, but there is hilarity, wisdom, and redemption along the way. No one but my father could cap the darkest, most honest moment in this story with a fart.

My father did with words what Fred Astaire did with his body, something out of this world that no one else could possibly pull off. Even as an old man my dad defied gravity and did the audacious thing of creating something out of nothing.

Nanette Vonnegut

Basic Training

A Novella

I.

"In many ways, Haley, this is the nicest room in the house, even though it is little and has only one window," said Annie Cooley, a woman in her middle twenties. She sat on the edge of the cot, her heavy legs crossed, and watched her sixteen-year-old cousin unpack his small suitcase. "The view of the elm grove and the duck pond is very good, and you'll have a lot more privacy than any of us in this end of the house."

Haley Brandon arranged his three white shirts in one corner of a deep bureau drawer, nodding absently at the end of each of Annie's sentences. He was tired after a fitful night aboard a railroad coach, and he was glad that Annie was content to talk on and on without calling upon him to contribute to the conversation. She was a complete stranger to him, and not a very interesting-looking one at that. He would not have known what to say to her, if it had been up to him to lead the talking. He was something less than adept at making new friends quickly, he thought uncomfortably. He glanced out of the window. Not even the land was remotely reminiscent of anything he had seen before.

"Now you take Kitty and Hope," Annie continued, referring to her younger sisters. "Their windows look right out on the new hog barn and the tool shed, and I've got the silo to look at." She grimaced, and two deep dimples appeared in her plump cheeks. "I've really got the worst room of all. The walls are just like cardboard, and I'm right next to the General's room. He's moving around until all hours, so it's a wonder I get any sleep at all. And I'm the one who always has to get up first, too."

"You all call your father the General?" asked Haley.

"Oh, after the war, everybody around here called him that, and we just kind of picked it up, too. My sister Hope says it's because he's more like a general than a father, but that's just some of her mean smartiness. Nobody ever had a better daddy than we do." She nodded twice in affirmation of her statement.

"I would like to hang a picture over my bed," said Haley. "Would it hurt anything if I drove a nail in the wall?"

"Oh, I guess it would be all right, if you'd be very careful not to crack the plaster. But that's for the General to say, of course," said Annie. "You can ask him when you meet him at suppertime. He ought to be in a pretty good mood, because he figures he's got Caesar and Delores licked."

"More cousins?" Haley asked abstractedly. He was examining a framed photograph, which had been swathed in a pair of flannel pajamas in the heart of his suitcase.

Annie chuckled appreciatively. "Maybe you'll think they look like cousins when you see them tomorrow," she said. "Caesar and Delores are the horses who pull the wagon. They ran away with a load last week, and they tore up the vegetable garden before they finally came up against a fence. The General's out today, trying some new bits that look like bicycle chains with sawteeth along one edge. He says if those two get fancy with him again, he'll saw their heads off before they can run ten yards." She seemed to relish the picture. "That's why he wasn't here to welcome you this afternoon," Annie explained. "He's out driving the team himself to make sure they know who's boss now. Ordinarily, he only goes out and works on D-days."

"I'm afraid I don't know about D-days," said Haley politely.

"Didn't I explain all about that? Well, you would have seen all about it on the bulletin board anyway. Tuesdays and Thursdays are D-days, which means that everybody, including Kitty, Hope, and the General, has to go out and work a full day on the farm. Won't make much difference to you, I guess. I understand you're going to be working a full week. The only difference on D-days will be that you'll be on D-squad instead of C-squad. D-squad is the General, the two girls, you, and Mr. Banghart. Mr. Banghart is nuts. C-squad is you and Mr. Banghart."

"Uh huh."

"A- and B-squads are a couple of other crews. They're out working another part of the farm about a mile from here."

"Sounds a little like the Army," Haley ventured.

Annie rose from the cot with effort, smoothed her apron, and walked over to Haley's side. "It's the only way to get a lick of work out of anyone, organization is, according to the General," she said. She looked at the picture that was absorbing most of his attention.

"The glass on it got cracked somehow," he said. "Maybe I

could go into town and get another one. Do you suppose that would be possible?"

"Well, I don't know. You'll have to ask the General about that, too. He says you're going to be a pretty busy boy around here, and I imagine he'll want you to stick close to the farm for a while, anyway. Sometimes," she said bitterly, "the girls walk into town and leave me to make the beds, wash the dishes, and straighten up the house all by myself—like today. I suppose they could get you another glass, if you asked them, if they could leave off chasing boys long enough to do it." She studied the photograph. "Those your folks?"

"Yes, my mother and father," said Haley gravely. "This was taken when they were very young, of course. You can tell that by the way Mother's got her hair fixed. They somehow never had many pictures taken of themselves together. This is about the only one."

"They're both very nice looking," said Annie. She squinted so as to see the picture more sharply. "You'd never know that the General and your mother were brother and sister, except for maybe the lines around her eyes." She paused, and something like warmth came into her eyes for the first time since Haley had seen them. "Golly," she said, "I can imagine what you've been through. We lost our mother while the war was going on, you know, and I had to kind of try and take over. Believe me, I know how you feel, Haley."

Haley did not want to talk or think about it. He turned his back on her and busied himself with straightening the contents of his sock drawer.

"It's funny about relatives, isn't it?" mused Annie. "Here you are my first cousin, even if it is by adoption, and I never laid eyes on you before today, and the General's never seen you. I just wonder where Kitty and Hope and I'll be twenty years from today." She made clucking noises and shook her head slowly.

The sound of voices and the crunching of footfalls in the gravel driveway below brought Haley and Annie from their separate reveries.

"I'm good and sick of walking. You've got a license. Why don't you put your foot down and demand to use the car?" complained a girl's high, melodic voice.

"That's your cousin Hope," said Annie. "She's about your age."

"He'd re-enlist as a private first," said a second voice, with a gentle twang, pitched somewhat lower than the first. "If I got a speck of dust on it, I might as well stick my head in the oven and turn on the gas. Remember what he did to that poor pigeon?"

"That's your cousin Kitty," Annie explained. "She's a year older, and president of her sorority at the high school."

"You're going to have to do the dishes tonight. Roy is coming by for me at seven, dear," said Kitty's voice.

"Drop dead," said Hope.

"O.K., then let the mother hen do it again," said Kitty. The front door slammed, and the conversation stopped.

"I'm the mother hen," muttered Annie. "I have no doubt that they'll tell you a lot of kind things about me when my back is turned. They may not have been behind the door when God passed out the pretty faces, but Heaven only knows where they were when He divided up the gratitude."

Haley was embarrassed, not knowing what comment was expected of him. "I'm sure they're very nice," he said.

"You'll see, Haley; you'll see," said Annie with a crooked smile. She shuffled from the room to the head of the staircase and shouted down to Kitty and Hope. "You two girls get on your good behavior. Your cousin Haley's here a day early, and I want him to see what a fine, happy family he's getting into."

She returned to Haley's room, followed by Kitty, whose full hips swayed with studied grace as she crossed the bare floor to where Haley stood, his long fingers laced behind him, a fixed smile on his face.

"So this is Haley," Kitty exulted. Haley fidgeted under her warm, albeit vacant, gaze. Her face had much of the simple-naturedness of Annie's, but the setting of this attribute was altogether enchanting, he thought. One year his senior, she was fully a woman, and her lush maturity made Haley feel very young and frail indeed.

His awe must have shown, for Kitty crooned, "Aw, look at him, Annie. What's the matter, youngster? Afraid of girls, or don't you like it out here in God's country?"

"I think I'll like it very much," stammered Haley. "My mother used to tell me about when she was a little girl out here, and I got to feel it was kind of a second home of mine, too."

"But what a come-down from New York, I'll bet—nightclubs, theaters, fancy stores, and everything."

"She's crazy to hear about New York," said Annie. "Four million men in New York."

"It was very different, certainly," said Haley, thoughtfully. "We always lived in apartments, and there were a lot of interesting people around all the time. Father loved it, naturally. It was the only kind of life for him. But Mother always said she belonged back here."

"Well, we'll be seeing a lot of each other for many years to come," said Kitty as she left the room. "You'll have to excuse me until supper—which had better be on time for a change, Annie dear."

Haley was agog. "She's very beautiful, isn't she, Annie?" he said.

"That isn't exactly news for around two hundred miles," said Annie. "The General says she's a lot smarter than some of the livestock in the neighborhood, too." She changed the subject abruptly. "I almost forgot to point out the General's welcome present." She indicated a pair of silver military brushes, which rested side by side on the otherwise barren dresser top. "If you want to keep on the right side of him, keep your hair brushed, don't be scared of him, and don't ask to use the car. That car's his pride and joy, and he doesn't trust anybody within ten feet of it. It used to belong to a German general, and there's not another car in the country that can touch it."

"That doesn't sound very difficult," laughed Haley.

"And remember," said Annie with severity, "no matter what he seems like at times, the General is one of the finest men alive. Now go downstairs and meet your cousin Hope. She's in the sunroom."

As Annie had promised, Haley found Hope in the sunroom, her quasi-adult figure clad in denim trousers and a man's shirt.

She was seated tailor-fashion on the broad sill of a bay window. When she looked up at him, he felt as though his bones would melt. Her face was angelic beneath a honey-colored blizzard of close-cropped curls. The thoughtful depths of her dark green eyes, and the radiant cast of her features, dispelled in an instant the image of Kitty that Haley had thought would be foremost in his thoughts for the rest of his life. "Welcome to Ardennes Farm," she said. "It's good to have another young person around. This place needs young ideas like nobody's business."

"I didn't know the farm had a name," said Haley.

"Oh, yes," said Hope wearily, "it's in honor of a battle, just like everything else around here."

"Annie said you were very pretty, and you are," said Haley, astonishing himself with his atypical gallantry, and with the sudden affection for Hope that surged within him.

"Uh huh," said Hope, and Haley guessed that she hadn't heard him clearly, for her head was turned away from him, her gaze intent on what Haley perceived to be a horse-drawn wagon, which was making a fitful and noisy approach toward the house. "Look at that idiot, that big, childish, old fool, Haley," she said irritably.

As the wagon drew nearer, Haley saw that it was not moving continuously but was making a quick series of starts and stops, and that the man at the reins was standing on the empty wagon bed, dancing an abbreviated jig, and shouting at the top of his lungs. "Giddyap! by golly; whoa! by golly; giddyap! blast you; whoa! blast you . . ." A pink froth wreathed the mouth corners of the stamping, rearing horses.

Hope jumped through the open window onto the lawn below and ran toward the wagon, waving her arms. She reached it when it was less than one hundred yards from where Haley stood squinting into the bright, level rays of the setting sun. He watched with admiration Hope's courage and vigor, and with melancholy reflections of his own deficiency in those manly qualities, as she scrambled onto the wagon, stamped on it with fury, and berated the man at the reins.

"What do you want to do, kill the poor horses with those awful bits?" Haley heard her say.

"I'm darn well going to have the most obedient pair of horses in the state; *that's* what I'm trying to do," bellowed the driver. "Now get back in the house and set the table or something!" He was short and plump, something like Annie, Haley thought, and he wore a disheveled ten-gallon hat, whose limp brim fluttered in the wind from the south, occasionally slapping at his steel-rimmed spectacles as he argued. "Now get! Go on and get! Giddyap! by golly." The wagon jolted forward ten feet. "Whoa!" The driver hauled back on the reins.

Hope dropped from the wagon, ran to the head of the frantic team, and unsnapped the reins from the bridles. "You'll regret that piece of high-handedness, young lady," threatened the driver, pink with anger. In another moment, she had freed the team from the tongue and traces and set them trotting toward the barnyard.

Haley gaped as the man seized Hope by the arm and fetched her a smart slap on her behind. "Didn't hurt," she yelled. The man, still grasping her arm, marched her toward the house.

"Don't care, don't care, don't care," she chanted, as they scuffled nearer and nearer to Haley.

"We'll see who cares," said the man. He thrust her before him into the sunroom. Haley instinctively ducked behind a chair. "Now go upstairs, Miss I-know-so-much-more-than-anybody. No supper for you tonight, and no movies for a month. Do we understand each other?"

"Simply don't care at all," said Hope. She turned and walked turtle-slow to the foot of the stairs. "I repeat," she said, "that I don't care. I might add that this must have looked simply wonderful to cousin Haley, who's hiding behind the red chair."

The man wheeled to glare at Haley's shelter. Haley bobbed up from behind the chair's high back and bared his teeth in what he hoped would look like a smile. "How do you do, sir," said Haley.

"You're Haley Brandon?"

"Yessir."

"Well, how do you do, young man? I'm your uncle, the great big bad bully the girls call 'the General.' Welcome to Ardennes Farm, and what were you doing behind the chair? Did I scare you, eh?" The General chuckled jovially.

Haley smiled sheepishly. "I just didn't want to intrude—"

"Sorry about that disturbance," the General interrupted. "It's the sort of thing that could happen in any family—maybe not quite as often," he added thoughtfully. "You saw it all from the first?"

"Yessir."

"Good. Then I don't have to justify my actions. You saw the

outrage that gave me no alternative." He dismissed the matter with a shrug. "Well, first let me say that we're glad you're here. My sister brought you up as her own, and that's what I intend to do. I know a good bit about you already from your mother's letters. You're thinner than I expected—a whole lot thinner—but otherwise she kept me pretty well posted. She was a lot better letter writer than I am. I know you're quite a piano player, for one thing, and that you were looking forward to going to Chicago to study at the Conservatory this winter, before all this happened. That right?"

"Yessir, it is. I—"

"Good for you. If there's anything I admire in a man, it's ambition. Frankly, wanting to be a piano player seems like a funny one to me, but, like I've told the girls a million times, 'I don't care what you want to be, just as long as it's honest, and you want to be the best there is.' I think maybe we can send you to Chicago, all right."

Haley broke into his first heartfelt smile of the interview.

"I've heard you're pretty smart all the way around, too," the General continued. He settled into a chair and lit a cigarette. "Here you are sixteen, and you've already finished up high school. Wish you'd give some of your brains to Kitty. Looks like she'll be in high school until the diamond jubilee of the atom bomb." He motioned for Haley to sit down. "I hope you haven't got a swelled head about your school record."

"I just liked school was all," said Haley, blushing, "and I went to summer school. I don't think I'm any smarter than—"

"Don't say Kitty," warned the General. "I was just going to tell you a story about a man I grew up with, just in case you were cocky about being smart in school. I see you aren't, but I'll tell it to you anyway. I learned a lot from what happened to him."

"I'd like very much to hear about it," said Haley.

"Well, Haley, this boyhood chum of mine was a lot like you, from what I've heard about you. He was always reading books, books, books—everything he could get his hands on. We used to ask him to come fishing or to play baseball, and things like that, and he always had the same answer: 'No thanks, I just got a new book that looks very interesting.' Sometimes he'd forget to stop reading for meals. By the time he was fifteen, he knew more about the royal family of Siam and the slum problem in Vladivostok than I knew about the back of my hand. All his teachers swore he was a genius, and said he'd be at least President of the United States when he was thirty-five." He paused to give Haley a meaningful look.

Haley attempted to appear as solemn and absorbed as possible. "What finally became of him?" he asked soberly.

The General seemed satisfied that his story was carrying the proper impact. "When World War II broke out, this man was immediately made an officer. Everybody expected him to win the war single-handedly. But when the going got tough over there in France, he cracked up completely. It turned out he didn't know the first thing about leadership, and he couldn't even take care of himself, so he was sick all the time." The General lowered his voice. "The morale in his company was so bad that all his men had thrown away their gas masks rather than carry them on marches. The first thing you know, the Jerries dropped mustard-gas shells all over them. Zip! One whole company wiped out! And I'll always say it was a library card that killed them. See my point?"

"Yessir, I think so. He was one-sided. Is that it?"

"That's it in a nutshell," said the General, beaming. "You expressed it perfectly. That's why I brought my whole family out here to the farm to live after the war, to keep us all from getting soft, from getting one-sided. Now spruce up for supper. People with dirty fingernails don't get to eat around here."

II.

At 2 a.m. Central Standard Time, as reckoned by the parlor mantel clock in the home of Brigadier General William Cooley, retired, a light beam left the burning sun. At 2:08 it glanced from the lip of a moon crater, and a second later died on earth, in the staring eyes of Haley Brandon.

Haley lay sleepless between cool sheets, his thin arms folded behind his head, his eyes fixed on the window through which the wistful moonlight streamed. He felt wholly a stranger. None of the old, seemingly sweetly reasonable patterns of the past now applied. He was not actively melancholy—it was too soon for that. Rather, he was like a settler on his first day in a foreign land, bemused by his initial contacts with unfamiliar customs, not yet ready to admit that it would be those customs instead of his own that would enable him to remain and prosper.

"We'll see to it that you earn your way as best you can—with good, old-fashioned work. Sounds harsh, maybe, but you'll thank us for it in later years. We'll put some meat on you, too," the General had said at supper. The sweat- and sinew-worship that seemed to pervade life at Ardennes Farm was a great curiosity to Haley. *Robust* was the password. As a Manhattan cliff-dweller, he had won the loyalty of his small circle of friends—most of them adults and fellow musicians—with the cleverness of his fingers on a piano keyboard, with his promise as a concert pianist. Now, he reflected, the emphasis had been changed to the cleanliness of his fingers, to whether he could move a piano.

Haley thought about the peculiar man into whose hands he had been delivered for guidance. The General, he knew from having heard his mother talk about him, was a competent manager, a brave soldier, and well off financially, though not given to exhibiting the last-named quality. He had taken over management of the old Cooley farmstead, run by tenants for nearly a generation, after his retirement from the Army. Haley remembered a few discussions between his mother and father as to the truth of his mother's contention that the General, "down deep," had a heart of gold. His mother had never been able to produce much evidence for the affirmative. His father, on the other hand, had always had dozens of incidents to recall, which seemed to back up his opinion that the General was a "pompous, selfish old teddy bear with sawdust for brains." As he lay abed for his first night in his new home, Haley thought he liked the General. The man was gruff, certainly, but he always gave sound reasons for the things he did.

Haley flexed his fingers and recalled the dreamlike quality his music had given his life in the past; and a pleasurable shudder passed over him as he reminded himself that that part of his life would begin anew in thirty days—for the General had promised that he might go to Chicago to resume his studies then. That was all that really mattered, Haley decided. Knowing that that much of the future was assured, he decided that he could adjust to any of the new order's rigors and get along with just about anyone.

It was certainly to the General's credit as a man of compassion that he should understand the importance of music to his new charge, Haley thought, for the man was as tone-deaf as a sparrow, and so were two of his three daughters. Judging from the whistling and humming they did, he had concluded that only Hope was able to carry a tune. Haley had heard that this was a hereditary trait. His mother, or, as Annie had reminded him, his foster mother, had been similarly afflicted. In this thought Haley found some consolation for his not being a blood relative of the Cooleys. There were apparently no instruments on the farm, and the evening's choice of radio programs had indicated that the General and his family found homicide far more entertaining than music. As Haley had undressed for bed, he had been surprised to hear an excellent, if untrained, tenor voice singing hymns in the barn, and he had wondered who it might have been. It could not have been a Cooley, at any rate. He decided to ask about it in the morning.

Tomorrow his new life would begin in earnest in the vast, unfamiliar flatness of the plain—a world of strange sounds and sights and attitudes. He was, the General had said, to help with the haying.

He turned over, pulled the sheet over his head, and closed his eyes. Haley dreamed of saying good night to his mother and father, of wishing them, handsome and young in evening clothes, a pleasant time at their party. He dreamed of the friends who had come to get him the next morning, to tell him that he must stay with them for a little while, that there had been an automobile accident, that he mustn't cry, that he must be a man. . . . He had cried.

III.

Haley was awakened the next morning by a banging on his door, a shout by his ear, and the shock of a cold washcloth on his face. He sat upright and saw the General standing at the foot of the cot, squat, fat, and laughing. A towel was knotted about the man's abdomen; with another he was rubbing his bare chest to a glowing pink. "You're not in the music business, boy; you're a farmer now. Take a cold shower, and be down for breakfast in ten minutes, or you don't eat," he trumpeted.

"Yessir," said Haley. Ten minutes later he was seated, puffing and shivering, at the long kitchen table, ducking his head now and then to avoid the flying elbows of Annie, who was energetically making flapjacks on the range behind him. The hot water faucet in the shower stall had been a cruel fraud, he reflected resentfully. The glare from the naked bulb that hung over the table hurt his eyes. He looked away from it to the blackness outside the windows and realized with sleepy awe that he would be seeing a sunrise for the first time in his life. "Good morning," he said, after waiting fruitlessly for someone—Annie, Hope, or the General—to acknowledge his presence.

The General and Hope sat across the table from him. Both gave him cursory nods. Hope's expression was sullen, and the General's boisterous spirits of a few minutes ago seemed to have fled. Haley supposed that they were still nourishing the unpleasantness of the previous afternoon. Uncomfortable in that sort of silence, Haley tried to break it again. "It's a nice morning," he said.

The General looked up. "Brush your teeth this morning, boy?"

"Yessir."

"Good," said the General firmly. "Dirtiest place in the world, next to the fingernails, the human mouth is."

"Speak for yourself," muttered Hope. Haley was grateful that only he seemed to have heard her. The General gave no sign, devoting his full attention to the flapjacks Annie had placed before him. As had been the case at supper the night before, the General was the first to be served. Haley gathered that it was customary not to talk during breakfast.

As he gulped the last of his strong, black coffee, the back door opened, and a muscular, black-haired man, apparently in his thirties, entered. His clothes were threadbare denim, but his manners were wonderfully courtly, Haley thought, and his grooming faultless. His face was shaved and scrubbed to the luster of wax apples, and his heavily pomaded hair resembled a patent-leather helmet. He crossed the room to a chair next to the range, made a brief bow to each person at the table, and sat down.

"Annie'll get you some coffee, Mr. Banghart," said the General. "By the way, you haven't met my nephew, have you? Mr.

Banghart, this is Haley Brandon. You two will be working to-gether as C-squad on Mondays, Wednesdays, Fridays, and Sat-urday mornings."

Haley and Mr. Banghart rose and shook hands. "A pleasure, I'm sure," said Mr. Banghart.

"Pleased to meet you," said Haley. "Are you by any chance the man who was singing in the barn last night?"

"The same. Did you enjoy it?"

"You have an awfully good voice, I think," said Haley.

Mr. Banghart, who had dropped Haley's hand, startled him by grabbing it again and squeezing it hard. "That's the first kind word anybody's ever had for me," he said solemnly.

"That's simply not so," said the General, in a half-laughing, patronizing tone.

Mr. Banghart ignored him. "I'd be glad to sing for you any time," he said to Haley. "What would you like to hear?"

Haley was startled by the reaction his pleasantry had started. He had never before set a man seething with gratitude, and the situation confused him. "'Rock of Ages' is very nice," he said at last, recalling that Mr. Banghart had done justice to this hymn the night before.

Mr. Banghart's lungs swelled like blacksmiths' bellows, and the room was filled with his powerful singing voice. Haley took a step backward. The General hammered on the table. "Not dur-ing breakfast!" he bawled above the singing, as though he were commanding a regiment.

Mr. Banghart stopped his singing immediately. "Now *you're* against me," he said reproachfully.

"Oh, for Heaven's sake, I am not against you," said the General irritably, "but I certainly will be if you do *that* again."

"Sorry," said Mr. Banghart, "but more for your sake than for mine." He shrugged and resumed his seat by the range.

"All right, all right," said the General soothingly. He looked up at the clock and fidgeted. "Now where's that Kitty?" he said. "What time did she get in last night, Annie?"

"Three in the morning," said Annie, handing Mr. Banghart his coffee. "She was out with that Roy Flemming again," she added. Haley saw Hope glare at her sister.

"That's the end, the absolute end," said the General. "You can tell her, when she gets up, that every minute after six that she slept is one weekend night that she has to stay in. You can also tell her that Mr. Flemming and his motorcycle are no longer welcome at Ardennes Farm. Put that on the bulletin board," he ordered.

Annie nodded in agreement. "Good," she said.

"Know where the bulletin board is?" the General asked Haley.

"I think I saw it there in the sunroom. Is that it, sir?"

"That's it, allrighty. You just watch the bulletin board. Annie keeps it up for me, and it'll help you stay out of mischief. Your name appeared on it for the first time today."

"What did it say about me?" asked Haley, with a trace of anxiety.

"You get up at 5 sharp, take a cold shower, brush your teeth for two minutes, pick up your pajamas and hang them on the hook inside the closet door; eat breakfast, go help with the haying; eat lunch, go out and hay some more; eat supper, listen to the radio for an hour, brush your teeth for two minutes, take a cold shower, hang up your clothes, and go to bed. Every minute's accounted for," said the General proudly. He looked again at the kitchen clock. "H-hour," he announced, and D-squad marched out into the vermilion sunrise.

By 11 a.m., the wagon was stacked high with the day's sixth load of hay. The hay, the General had explained to Haley, had been pounded and bound into bales by a machine that had passed over the field the day before. The dense bundles were as high as Haley's chest, weighed about half of what he imagined Hope to weigh, and were as wide and thick as the General's middle. There was room for three more bales on top. Haley hung his baling hook on a wheel spoke, swept away the sweat that streamed into his eyes, and begged for a rest.

"You just had a rest period, Haley," said the General. "You'll find you won't get tired as quickly if you keep at it steadily. Breaking up your rhythm with rest periods all the time, no wonder you're pooped. You'll never get your second wind that way." He was atop the load, reins in hand, with Hope seated beside him, her legs dangling over the side.

Haley shook his head wearily and sat down on the ground, panting, wishing to Heaven that the nightmare of heat, creeping time, and lamed muscles would end. "I'll be all right in a minute, I guess—soon as I get my breath," he said. Mr. Banghart, who had been working on the opposite side of the wagon, walked over to him and told him to climb onto the wagon, that he would finish the load.

"Let him learn to pull his own weight, Mr. Banghart," warned the General. "He can do it. Come on, boy, three to go."

Limply, painfully, Haley sank his hook into a nearby bale. He worried it along the ground to the wagon. Hope waited, hook poised, for him to swing it upward to where she could catch it and drag it into place.

"Put your back into it, boy," shouted the General, and Haley swung the bale. Hope made a grab for it, but missed, for it was a full yard beyond her hook. Haley staggered backward under the weight, his eyes and lungs filled with the dust and splinters that showered down from the bale. His feet tangled, and he fell hard on the sharp stubble, the bale on top of him.

He was yanked to his feet at once by Mr. Banghart, who, with his mouth close to Haley's ear, whispered, "Don't you worry— we'll take care of that old devil when the right time comes. Wait and see."

Haley rubbed his smarting eyes and brought into focus the face of Hope, who was rocking from side to side with laughter. He felt utterly humiliated standing before her, comical in his weakness, and in his clothing—cast-off work clothes of the General, too short, too wide, high on his ankles and wrists, bunched at his waist. Exhaustion and sudden loneliness billowed in his narrow breast. He sank to the ground again.

The General eased himself down from his perch and stood over him, kicking gently at the soles of his shoes and chiding, "Come on, boy, get up. All right, get up." Haley stood. The General seemed more embarrassed than angry. "That's enough of that," he said. "Mooning and malingering will get you nowhere around here, do you understand? I'm ashamed of you."

"Leave him alone," Haley heard Hope call.

Blushing and apologizing in half-soliloquy, Haley clambered atop the wagon, unable to look at Hope. Mr. Banghart swung three more bales up to Hope, and the wagon moved, jolting and creaking, toward the barnyard.

In the still, dry heat of the loft, under a tin roof too hot to touch, Hope, Haley, and Mr. Banghart dragged bale after bale from the wagon over the splintered floor to a growing stack deep in the shadows of one end. The General remained on the wagon to steady the horses. Tormenting himself, Haley tried to imagine what the others were thinking of him. Hope was the only one he really cared about. The two of them worked together, their hooks driven into the same bale. She said nothing, concentrating her attention on the hard work to be done. He was bewildered by the effect her presence had had upon him since the first instant he had seen her. He now found her more beautiful than ever, with her hair lightened by dust, and with heat bringing her loose clothes into conformity with the lines of her young figure.

Mr. Banghart rolled a cigarette, politely excused himself, and went out into the barnyard to smoke it. The General joined him with a cigar, leaving Haley and Hope alone in the barn. Haley sat down on a bale next to Hope. "Don't worry about it. You'll get used to farmwork after a while," she said. "We all did. Takes about a month."

For want of a rational comment on this message, Haley changed the subject. "Mr. Banghart is a funny one," he said. "I never knew anyone to talk to himself so much."

Hope giggled. "He's got a screw loose, all right, but the General says he's the best worker we ever had on the farm," she said.

"Try and hear what he talks to himself about sometime. It's all about what he's going to do to people he thinks are out to get him—which is practically everybody. You're lucky—he liked you right away, and that's unusual." She became more thoughtful. "I shouldn't laugh. It's kind of sad about him, I guess."

"Has he ever done anything to anybody?" asked Haley uneasily.

"Oh, no, he just talks about it. He has one of the tenants' houses all to himself, and he spends most of his spare time there. He never goes into town, and the General has him working by himself, or with us, so there isn't much chance for him to get into trouble with anybody."

"Is he married? What does he do with his money?"

"As far as we know, he's a bachelor, but he keeps that house cleaner than a woman would. The General thinks he's got his money hidden in the house somewhere, because he never goes anywhere where he could spend it. We do all his shopping for him, and he never buys anything but food and tobacco and pad-locks," Hope explained matter-of-factly. "That's the really funny thing about him—the locks. If you make a trip into town, chances are he'll ask you to get him one. He's got padlocks all over that house. There were four on his front door the last time I counted."

The General called from below, "Lunch time!" To Haley the announcement was incredible. At 9 a.m., after watching four rural hours inch by, he had concluded that the clocks of Ardennes Farm were lubricated with molasses, and that noon was still a century away in terms of time as he had known it in the city.

Noon brought with it the solid blessings of strong coffee and whole milk, of strawberry jam and biscuits, of ham and gravy. It was an hour of peace and plenty, reminding Haley of a medieval custom he had read about—whereby a condemned man was hanged and skillfully revived several times before being permitted to expire completely. The analogy did not spoil his appetite. He wolfed his food, excused himself, and lay down on the sunroom couch.

Bits of conversation from the kitchen infiltrated his consciousness. He stored them away, too weary to think much about them. Kitty, who, Annie had said, had slept until 11, was defending her relationship with Roy Flemming, her beau of the night before. She seemed agitated, punctuating her replies to the General's poignant assaults on Roy's character with nose blowing. She declared that she loved Roy, and that this was one romance her father was *not* going to break up. There seemed to have been plenty of cases where the General had succeeded in doing just that.

"Until you're twenty-one, young lady, let me be the judge of who your associates should be," Haley heard the General say. "After that, you're free to marry anybody, simply anybody— Flemming, Mr. Banghart, or the next bum who stops for a handout. Until that happy day, however, I am very much in charge. Do we understand each other?" Kitty hastened past Haley's aching form and hurried up the stairs to slam her bedroom door on a loveless world for lovers.

"H-hour!" shouted the General, and he harangued his flagging troops into the field once more.

In an eon came evening, to cool and to displace the sounds of daytime with whispers and croaks and sounds like rusty hinges from grass-tuft sanctuaries in woods and pastures and from lily pads a quarter of a mile away.

Annie had prepared supper an hour ago, and, from the small window at the end of a long corridor between bales in the loft, Haley could see her putting it into the oven to keep it warm. He, Hope, and Mr. Banghart, meeting a quota set by the General, were stacking the last wagonload in the barn. The General had returned to the house, leaving the three of them to handle what remained without his supervision. It was much cooler now, and, with him gone, an element of playfulness came into the business of lugging bales. Haley found his burdens miraculously lightened. Mr. Banghart sang a medley of rhythmic spirituals, setting a tempo by which they tugged and lifted. The work was done.

They sat down in the corridor between bales to get their breaths and to shake the dust and straw-bits from their hair. As bad as his first taste of rural life had been, Haley found himself looking with pride at the results of their labor, stacked bales rising like skyscrapers on either side of them. Mr. Banghart sat still for only a minute, arising again to feel along the upper surface of a rafter until he found what he wanted, a flashlight. "We can show Haley our secret, can't we, Hope?" he asked.

"I suppose so. It's really kind of silly, though."

"I'd like very much to see it. I wouldn't tell anybody," Haley promised.

They led him down the corridor to within a few feet of the window at its end. The bales had been stacked here before

Haley's arrival at Ardennes Farm. Mr. Banghart pointed his flashlight at a bale in the bottom row. "Notice anything different about that one?" he asked.

"Well, there's a piece of cloth tied around the baling wire," said Haley.

"That's a marker," said Mr. Banghart. "Try and move that one."

Haley tugged at the bale dutifully. He was surprised to find that it slid from its place easily, that the bales above did not rest upon it.

"It's a tunnel!" Mr. Banghart announced happily. He dropped onto all fours and crawled into the opening and out of sight.

"Go on in, Haley," said Hope. "There's nothing to be afraid of."

Haley followed Mr. Banghart into the dark passage, finding that there was barely room in which to squirm. After snaking his way through nine feet of the snug, airless tunnel, with claustrophobia beginning to give him twinges of panic, he found himself in a chamber in which he could stand, lighted by Mr. Banghart's flashlight. It was a room hollowed in the stacked bales, as long and wide as the sunroom couch, with a ceiling, resting on planks, that barely brushed the top of his head.

Hope emerged from the passage as he stood blinking in disbelief. "This is one place where the General and Annie can never find you," she said. "And there'll be times when you'll be glad there is such a place." She sat down in a corner. "It was just a crazy thing to do to break the monotony, but it's a good job, if I do say so myself. I'm the architect; Mr. Banghart's the builder. Like it?"

"It's a fine job," said Haley, impressed.

"A fellow likes to get away from it all now and then," Mr. Banghart observed thoughtfully. They sat in silence for a few minutes, digesting this wisdom. Mr. Banghart spoke up again. "Want to know another secret?" he whispered. There was no need for whispering, Haley thought, with the walls three yards thick.

"Certainly we want to know another secret," said Hope. "Let's have it."

Mr. Banghart reached inside his faded shirt, bringing forth a long leather sheath. He drew from the sheath a double-edged hunting knife, with a blade the length of his hand. He twisted it before his eyes slowly—affectionately, Haley thought—and its bright surfaces sent flecks of light racing along the walls. "It's so sharp I can shave with it," he said, running a moistened finger over the edge. "Honed it for two hours last night." He smiled proudly. "Now I'm ready for anything."

"You wouldn't really use it on somebody," said Haley, making an effort to appear as undisturbed by the knife as Hope seemed to be. Though he managed to keep his voice casual, he was wishing that he had not settled in the corner farthest from the tunnel, with Mr. Banghart between him and the outside world.

"Oh, wouldn't I use it, though?" said Mr. Banghart. He jabbed the blade into a bale. "Wouldn't I, though? Let me tell you something, Haley: If they want to play rough, so can I."

Haley looked questioningly at Hope and caught her laughing quietly at his discomfort. He remembered that when he had quizzed her about Mr. Banghart's hallucinations of a world out to get him, she had shrugged them off as being amusing and nothing more. "I think we'd better go to supper," Haley murmured.

Hope agreed and started for the tunnel. Mr. Banghart did not budge but continued to stare at the blade. Hope nudged him gently to break his fascination. The flashlight slipped from his hand to bang on the floor and go out.

The shock of sudden darkness released Haley's dammed-up fear. He plunged toward the tunnel, driving with every bit of strength in his legs. His shoulder struck something soft, and he heard Hope cry out in anger. He wriggled into the passageway and made his way to the corridor in a few seconds, emerging breathless and badly scratched by the splintery floor. He was almost to the loft ladder before realization of what he had done broke his frantic stride. Worse than leaving Hope to defend herself, he had knocked her aside in order to save his own skin.

Fear and conscience struggled for mastery of his feet. Conscience gained an almost imperceptible advantage, and Haley found himself returning slowly to the tunnel. In his hand was a claw hammer he had found by the ladder.

His rescue mission was frustrated, his honor unredeemed. He was met in the corridor by Hope, who was massaging her right arm, and by Mr. Banghart, whose knife was sheathed and tucked beneath his belt.

"What on earth got into you, all of a sudden?" asked Mr. Banghart solicitously.

"I tripped and fell in the dark," said Haley quickly. He turned to Hope and prayed that his lie would make him whole again in her eyes. "I'm sorry, Hope. I didn't mean to fall against you."

She shrugged. "Couldn't be helped, I guess. Don't worry about it—just a bruise."

Haley sighed gratefully. They descended the ladder and walked from the barn together. Mr. Banghart struck out for his own house, and Haley and Hope mounted the back steps to the kitchen. Just before she pushed open the screen door, Hope turned to Haley, who was congratulating himself on having talked his way out of a perfectly desolate situation.

"If you flop as a piano player, you can always make a good living as a bodyguard," she said.

IV.

"Now take the case of the 240 howitzer," said the General. "Far more effective against concrete bunkers than aerial bombardment. I remember just before the Bulge, the glamour boys dropped everything they had on a Jerry pillbox, and they didn't even chip it. So I called back to First Army Headquarters. 'Send up some 240s,' I said. Well, sir, . . ."

Haley nodded and turned his face toward the sunroom windows to hide his yawn from the General. Nothing moved in his line of sight save Mr. Banghart, who bobbed in the distance on the springing seat of a moving machine, circling again and again a shrinking island of standing alfalfa. It was Saturday afternoon—an afternoon, as the bulletin board decreed, for "recreation and cleanup." Haley had tuned in a concert broadcast on the sunroom's small radio, but when the General had started to shout war stories above the music, Annie had turned it off. From overhead came a muffled scuffing as Kitty and Hope moved about their rooms, tidying them up. Annie sat in a rocker near Haley, attentive to the General's words and seemingly very entertained.

Haley wondered if he should tell the General about Mr.
Banghart's knife. Hope had made him promise not to say anything about it. She had laughed the matter off and repeated what
he had heard from others on the farm, that Mr. Banghart was no
more dangerous than the mice in the corncrib. Still and all, he
reflected, the combination of jangled brains and an eight-inch
bowie knife would be reassuring to very few persons. But the last
thing he wanted to do was to go against Hope's judgment. . . .

"I told Banghart to quit at noon, and he got surly with me,"
said the General as an aside, apparently seeing that Haley's attention had wandered from the turning point of World War II to
the distant Mr. Banghart.

"He didn't even stop for lunch," said Annie.

"Too bad it's just the nuts that work that hard," said the General.
"Seems like he does something like this every time the tempera-
ture gets above ninety. Remember the time he had the manure-
spreader out until midnight? *That* was a hot day." The General
snickered. "Boy, the farm help you get these days. The darnedest
thing happened this morning. I went over to the hog barn to
watch Banghart feed the pigs. For no reason at all, he got sore as
the devil when he saw me. He threw down the bucket, and can
you imagine what he said?"

"I can't imagine. What did he say?" said Annie. Haley noted
with distaste that her conversations consisted mainly of questions
of this sort, and of echoes.

"He told me that I was going to cross him up once too often
and get mine along with the rest of them. Can you imagine?" The
General was laughing.

"Maybe you'd better get rid of him," Haley blurted.

The General looked at him with surprise. "I'd sooner get rid of the tractor. He's nothing to worry about. I've got him right under this." The General held up a broad, flat thumb and winked. "Well, where was I? Oh, yes. 'Send me up some 240s,' I said, and . . ."

Haley's thoughts strayed again, taking him back to the events of lunchtime, when Roy Flemming, Kitty's current love, had appeared in the kitchen, having walked into the house without knocking. Haley had never seen anything quite like Roy before. His red hair, his freckled moon-face and childish blue eyes were familiar enough, but his bearing and thin mustache seemed as out of keeping with these as an olive in the bottom of a milkshake. Haley wondered just what Roy imagined himself to represent. His swagger and attire—gleaming riding boots, enormously wide belt spangled with bits of colored glass, crushed and twisted Army officer's hat, and polo shirt decorated with palm trees—might be proper, Haley decided, for the leader of a bandit band in a musical comedy.

The General had spoken to Roy without looking up from his food. "Get out," he had said. Kitty had told Roy to sit down, that her father was joking. The General had thereupon offered to fill his "smart young behind with bird-shot" if he showed up again.

Roy had started to back out of the room, embarrassed, and bereft of all save the glittering trappings of his devil-may-care role. Kitty had dragged him back into the kitchen. "Tell him what you came for," Kitty had said. Roy had managed to clear his throat several times, and that was all.

"Well?" the General had said.

"Sir, your daughter and I want to get married, sir," Roy had said at last.

"I'd see her first in Hell," the General had said. He had stamped his foot suddenly, and Haley had jumped. "Scat!" Roy Flemming had fled.

Haley's recollection faded as the General's voice lifted from a monotone to a loud staccato. He was imitating the crash of 240 howitzer shells on a doomed German pillbox. "Ker-wham! Ker-wham! Kerwham! After an hour of that—kerwham!—we sent the Second Battalion in—rattattattatat—and there wasn't a Jerry left to fire a shot." The General chuckled. Annie snickered appreciatively, and Haley forced a smile.

"And then there was the time at Aachen, when the Jerries were using a church steeple for an observation post," the General began afresh. His back was to the doorway, and he twisted around in his chair to see what it was behind him that was distracting his audience. Kitty stood in the doorway. "Hello, dear," he said to her, in a kindly tone. "I hope you've gotten over any ill feelings you may have had against your old father."

"I'm going to marry him, and that's that."

The General shrugged. He took her hand and gave it an affectionate squeeze. "What do you want to do—mother a race of super-idiots? He can't concentrate on anything but his motorcycle for more than twenty seconds at a time. If you two were married and down to your last five dollars, he'd blow it on two foxtails and a chromium-plated exhaust-pipe extension. If it came to a choice between you or the motorcycle, sister, you'd lose."

"He's brilliant," declared Kitty. "He knows more about motors than anybody. And, while we're getting mean about it, what about you? You're as much in love with that German limousine of yours as Roy is with his motorcycle."

Haley saw that this rankled the General a little. "That car," he said crisply, "is the only one of its kind in the world. It couldn't be replaced for thirty thousand dollars. Moreover, young lady, I *do* have other interests. Take away Roy's motorcycle, and he'd vanish. I could build a better man with an Erector set."

Kitty turned white with fury. "He's brilliant, and he's good looking, and he's a gentleman, and he's considerate, and he's from a good family, and he's—"

The roar of a motorcycle in the driveway cut her short. The front door slammed, and Roy Flemming marched into the sunroom. Haley saw that his movements were ponderous, imprecise, and that he brought with him a withering effluvium of whisky. "I know when I've been insulted," Roy said hoarsely, "and I don't have to stand for it, either. I don't care if you're King of the Universe, I still don't have to. Nope."

The General held his nose.

"So I've been drinking," said Roy, with a flourish of his hand. "S'matter of small importance in the face of that with which I have been faced with. I offer my heart to your daughter, and all I get from you is shame and abuse, that's all." He snapped his fingers. "I'm here to wake you all up, to get you out of your ruts."

The General gave an experimental sniff, winced, and held his nose again.

"Oh, I'm on to you," said Roy. "You're trying to use psychology on me by making me think my breath smells bad, so I'll get confused and forget what I wanted to say. I'm one jump ahead of you, mister."

"Can't be the septic tank," murmured the General.

"Could be your soul," said Roy hotly. "You don't bother to think; you just say no to everything." He squinted to bring the General into focus. "Well, I'm here to tell you that it won't work on the sun and the stars and the moon, and it won't work with love like Kitty's and mine, either."

The General arose, grasped Roy by the collar and a handful of trouser-seat, and propelled him to the front door. His expression was placid, patient. "You say you want to marry my daughter, and I say no," he explained, releasing Roy on the front porch. "I couldn't stop the sun and the moon and the stars, if I wanted to— but I expect to be quite effective in your particular case."

Haley heard Roy shout from his motorcycle as he sped away with an angry clashing of gears: "I'll be back!"

"That's not original with him, you know," commented the General, returning to the sunroom.

After dinner, seated on the kitchen steps, Haley outlined the conversation to Hope, who nodded thoughtfully and made him repeat portions of it. "Roy's right about the way he tries to solve everything by saying no," she sighed. "That's how he got to be a general, I guess, but he sure isn't much fun as a father."

"I'm sure he's got a very good heart and is just trying to do what he thinks best," said Haley.

"Who isn't?" Hope shrugged. "Don't get me wrong, Haley. We love him dearly, and I think he loves us, too, probably lots more than most fathers love their children. But golly, his idea of doing us a favor is to discipline us every time we turn around." A patch of light on the grass to their left, cast from Kitty's window above, disappeared. Hope and Haley looked up at the darkened window. "Going to bed early," said Hope. "Guess she'll cry herself to sleep tonight." Suddenly she motioned for silence. "Listen!"

Haley heard a rustling in the untended barberry hedge bounding the driveway. A figure separated from the shadows, and Haley recognized Roy, who looked as though he had been eluding bloodhounds for a week. He spoke hoarsely, and he was visible for only a minute—long enough to give them a note for Kitty, rumpled and moist from his perspiring hands. He retreated again into the hedge, and Hope ran upstairs with the message, leaving Haley alone on the kitchen steps. The light in Kitty's room flashed on again, and Haley turned his head to see her standing in the window, waving her hands and nodding. A moment later, he saw Roy head across the barnyard toward the highway, running between patches of shadows in a low crouch.

Hope returned, vibrant with excitement. "They're going to get married anyway, Haley—tonight!"

Haley laughed nervously and found himself without adequate comment.

"And the wonderful thing about it is that we get to see them elope!"

"I'd rather keep out of it," said Haley, his voice tinged with anxiety.

"Oh, but you can't," said Hope, enthusiastically. "You're absolutely crucial. They're going to use your window, because it's the farthest from the General's room."

"Good grief! What if she gets caught by Annie or the General on her way out through my room? That'd look dandy for me."

"Oh, the General will never find out how she got out. He won't find out she's gone until morning. She's making a dummy for her bed right now."

"All the same, I'd be happier if—"

"You *are* a mouse, aren't you?" said Hope.

Haley suddenly hated himself for his querulousness. "I didn't mean it *that* way," he objected lamely. "It's just that I want to make sure everything's planned just right, that's all."

They returned together, with Hope apparently mollified, into the brightly lit sunroom, where the General and Annie perused, respectively, the first and second sections of the evening paper, with an occasional and complacent "huh" or "ha."

At 3 a.m., Caesar, the chastened horse, kicked the side of his stall twice, perhaps in token retribution for the sawtoothed bits. The solid thumps carried to the ears of Haley, who threw back his covers and ran to the window. In the silent patch of blues and blacks below him, he saw Roy moving toward the house, staggering beneath the weight of a tall ladder. Roy stood the ladder upright and leaned it in toward Haley's windowsill. The ladder gathered speed as it fell toward the house, and Roy was without leverage to stop it as it threatened to hit the clapboard siding with a thundering whack. Haley leaned out and caught the ladder just before it hit, and his hand served as a cushion between it and the house. In spite of himself he cried out and jerked his hand, which stung smartly and bled.

Roy soon popped his colorful head into the window, and

Hope and Kitty slipped through the bedroom door, looking furtively over their shoulders and struggling with several large pieces of luggage.

"Who yelled?" whispered Hope angrily.

Haley appealed with his eyes to Roy for vindication, but Roy, florid and perspiring, was staring amazed at the baggage Kitty expected to carry away on the nuptial motorcycle. Haley guessed, from what little he knew of Roy, that the idea of spiriting his love away had delighted him, but that the mechanical difficulties inherent in the desperate venture now depressed him terribly. Haley counted seven separate pieces of luggage.

"Darling," whispered Kitty, throwing her arms about Roy's neck.

Roy received the embrace woodenly. "Gee whiz, Kitty, half that stuff won't even fit through the window, let alone fit in the saddle bags," he said forlornly.

"You said we might be on the road for ten days; right in black and white you said that."

"Sure, honey, but we aren't going in a moving van."

"Better get going while the going's good," warned Hope.

Kitty began to look rattled. "What're you taking?" she asked.

"Change of socks, change of underwear," said Roy.

"Here, take this one and beat it," urged Hope, handing Kitty a small bag.

"It's all packed according to a system," said Kitty helplessly. "And I thought it was so good, too. There's underwear in one, skirts in another, blouses and sweaters in that big one." She looked at the bag in her hand. "I forget what's in this one."

"Is that the one with your toothbrush?" asked Roy.

"It *could* be," said Kitty, apparently not at all sure.

"That's the one we want," said Roy, taking it from her. "Let's go!"

Kitty hesitated, looked longingly at the baggage she was going to have to abandon, then squirmed through the window and onto the ladder.

Haley, Hope by his side, listened to the lovers' conversation as they descended.

"I got you a new kidney belt for the trip," said Roy affectionately.

"I think this is the bag with the hankies and the stockings," said Kitty.

Kitty and Roy, stumpy, grotesque, long-shadowed figures as seen by Haley and Hope from the bedroom window, were absorbed by the shadows of the barn, reappeared for a moment as they crossed the fence into the elm grove, and were lost from sight for good. Haley and Hope heard the roar and backfire of the motorcycle starting on the highway, then its even rumble, then hum, as it carried Roy and Kitty to joy everlasting.

"Well, I never," said Annie, filling the door with her breadth, the more impressive for being sheathed in an orange, daisy-spattered bathrobe. Haley's heart pumped harder and faster as Annie scratched herself and blinked at them sleepily. "Well, I never," she repeated at last. "What's going on at this hour?"

"Haley's window wouldn't open, and he asked me to help him get it unstuck," said Hope.

Annie's gaze, more wakeful now, turned toward the window.

Haley closed his eyes. "What's that ladder and luggage doing there?" she demanded, taking a step forward. The drone of Roy's motorcycle was still audible, and, when Haley opened his eyes for an instant, he saw Annie's head cocked to one side, in an attitude of listening and incredulity. "She ran off with him, didn't she?" she cried.

"Hush!" hissed Hope, and the General stepped from the darkness of the hallway.

"Kitty's run off with Roy, and these two helped her," said Annie, livid. "What'll we do?"

The General breathed heavily, his eyes moving about the small room—from Annie, to the ladder and luggage, to Haley and Hope. "I'll see you two downstairs in the sunroom in fifteen minutes, on the dot," he said.

"You'll see," said Annie, and she followed the General down the hall.

Haley could hear the General dialing then shouting into the telephone. "He always yells into the telephone," said Hope. Haley sensed that some of her defiant poise was gone, that she was worried. "He's talking to the police," she said with awe. They lapsed into despondent silence until Hope's watch indicated that the time for their hearing had come.

The General was at his desk, his back to them. Annie sat on the edge of the couch, pouring two cups of coffee. She told them to sit down, and so they sat, with only their sins and the coffee's fragrance to contemplate for perhaps ten minutes. Haley examined the back of his hand, which had begun to ache from the ladder's blow. A long welt crossed the back of it, and the skin was broken in three places along the knuckles.

"I have a theory," the General began suddenly, "that every-body with any sense has a good idea of how he looks to others. Let's put it to a test, shall we?" His tone was polite, impersonal, like that of a lecturer, Haley thought. "Hope?"

"Yes?" Her voice was faint.

"You and I are pretty much strangers. You weren't much more than a baby when I went away to war, so we never did have much time to get to know each other." He paused to light a cigarette. "You don't like me because you think I'm a bully, that it's fun for me to push other people around."

"Noooo," objected Hope, tearfully. "I love you, Daddy, really I do."

"Don't doubt it. Never did. That's an entirely different matter."

Hope started to plead again, but the General cut her short by addressing Haley. "As for you, young man, I don't think I'm far from the mark when I say that you think I'm pretty funny, even though you are scared to death of me. I'm a joke, an old fool who can't forget for a minute that he was a general. Maybe it was your father who taught you that."

"Hardly, sir," said Haley, embarrassed, but at a loss as to how he might argue the point.

"Good—the cards are on the table," said the General. "In case you haven't figured out for yourselves just what I think of you, I'll clear that up, too. First of all, I'm fond of you both. I think you're too soft and spoiled for your own good. I want you to be happy, and I get no fun at all out of hurting you. But you're still children, and I'm supposed to take care of you to the best of my ability. If I can teach you one simple lesson, I'll have done a good job of it. You're evidently going to have to learn the hard way that your happiness for the rest of your lives depends on how well you fit yourselves into other people's plans, not vice versa, and on how willing you are to submit to the judgment of someone who knows more than you do. Am I right or wrong?"

"You're right," faltered Hope.

"Yessir," said Haley. The lesson sounded like an eminently reasonable one, easily committed to memory.

"What you have done tonight has hurt, not helped, all of us," said the General, "and poor, harebrained Kitty most of all. You'll see. Because you helped her run away with that crude, asinine chimpanzee, she is in for nothing but grief. We'll get her back, because she's too young to marry without my say so, but she'll never be the same again—because you didn't have the good sense to stop her. Am I right or wrong?"

"I didn't know what I was doing," moaned Haley. Hope remained silent.

"Do you feel I have stated the situation fairly, and that you have done something quite bad?" asked the General, his eyebrows arched.

Haley and Hope nodded.

"Very well, then, some kind of punishment is in order. Hope, Annie and I have decided that you should be sent away to some boarding school. I'll look into the matter tomorrow, and I'll pick one where you'll be watched carefully and kept in line. I think one of your big troubles has been the smart-aleck company you've been keeping at the high school."

"Daddy!" cried Hope.

"Haley, I have decided that for your own good you'd better not go to the Conservatory. You will work around the farm instead. I wouldn't class that as punishment, actually. It's the greatest kind of character training a man can get."

Haley did not believe it. He shut out the sound of the General's voice and nodded mechanically. It was hours later that a chill passed over him and he knew that the small parcel of dreams he had brought with him into his new home was hopelessly smashed.

"That is all. Good night," said the General, without rancor.

"But, Daddy," began Hope.

"I said good night."

Annie had sat quietly, nodding in agreement whenever the General had spoken. "Better go now," she said. She rose and shooed them from the room. "What in Heaven's name happened to your hand, Haley?"

"The ladder banged it. It doesn't hurt much."

"You come with me," said Annie. She took him up to the bathroom and painted his cuts with iodine. Involuntarily, Haley jerked back his hand. "Hurt?" asked Annie.

"A little," said Haley, sucking in air between his teeth.

"Fine," said Annie, plainly satisfied. "Shows it's doing some good."

V.

"Quite a ruckus last night, eh?" called Mr. Banghart to Haley above the rattling and creaking of the empty wagon on its way to the fields. Haley sat on the rear corner of the wagon, kicking dispiritedly at the fragile white heads of milkweeds lining the lane. He did not hear Mr. Banghart's question; his senses were turned inward, examining his conscience.

Annie had aroused him this morning and reminded him that he and Mr. Banghart were to work today, even though it was Sunday. The radio had predicted rain, she had said, and the hay bales would be too heavy to lift and too wet to store if they were not brought in before the downpour. The General and Hope still slumbered, and Annie had returned to bed after warming coffee left over from the night before and laying out a bowl of cold cereal and an orange for Haley's breakfast. He had met Mr. Banghart in the barn and done what he could to help harness Caesar and Delores. The coffee had purged him of his sleepiness, giving him in its stead a keen, tense wakefulness.

He was willing to admit that he had done a bad thing in

helping Kitty elope with the somewhat substandard Roy Flemming. He did, then, for his own good, as the General had said, deserve to be punished. But he searched his conscience in vain for a grain of remorse to justify the desolating punishment the General had promised. "When you punish somebody, you take something away from them that they want," he reasoned. "All I had in the whole wide world was my music, so that's what I lost—everything."

As he reviewed his condition again and again in the light of a spotless conscience, he found himself starting to derive from it the pungent, bittersweet pleasure of righteous indignation. Another thought, however, nagging on the fringes of his consciousness, soon came into view to spoil his pleasure. He lived again his ignominious flight from the secret room in the loft, and his abandoning of Hope, and his spirits tumbled into depths of recrimination.

He looked up at Mr. Banghart and wondered how he had found out about the turmoil of the night before. "Probably watched it all through the windows," he thought. "Hope said he did a lot of that."

"Horses seem pretty frisky this morning," said Mr. Banghart, tugging gently on the reins to slow the pace of Caesar and Delores. Haley stood up and walked to Mr. Banghart's side. He saw that the corners of the horses' mouths were raw, and that every pull on the edged bits made them swing their heads wildly from side to side.

Mr. Banghart took out his hunting knife and began shaving fat splinters from a wagon stake. The cuts were effortless, Haley noted, with a youngster's admiration for a keen edge. "There's a great day coming," his companion crooned. "There are a lot of people around who are going to be wishing they had been a lot nicer to old Bing." He winked and returned the knife to its case. "A man can stand so much and no more, and they're all going to have to learn *that* the hard way."

Haley asked to have a look at the knife. Mr. Banghart was hesitant. At last he handed it over, admonishing him to be careful. "It'd take your arm off quicker than you could say 'Jack Robinson,'" he said proudly. "You're the only one I'd ever let look at it except Hope," he added. He shook his head mournfully. "A fellow's in pretty sad shape when he can only trust two people, isn't he, now?"

Haley nodded and found himself wondering who it was that *he* could trust. Everyone seemed intent on worrying him into a pattern of their own making, rather than trying to understand what it might be like to be Haley Brandon. He wondered most about Hope. With discomfiting insight, he recognized that any attention she might have shown him was probably a subtle defiance of her father. "Like protecting Caesar and Delores from him," he thought ruefully.

When they set about flinging bales onto the wagon, the circle of Haley's thoughts grew smaller, with limits set at the hard work on hand. He was pleased to see that he was accomplishing nearly as much as Mr. Banghart. It was more a matter of rhythm than strength—swinging the bales several times, then giving them a hearty boost with a knee on their upward arcs. True, when the load was three bales high, pitches more hefty than Haley's were called for, but he was able to make himself useful by sitting atop the load and pulling the bales into place as Mr. Banghart tossed them.

"It's a load!" he cried, when the fifth tier was complete.

Mr. Banghart shook his head. "We'll stack her seven high and save time," he said.

"That'll be above the stakes," Haley warned.

"I've done it a million times," said Mr. Banghart. "Nothing to it. Just drive easy, that's all."

Haley looked dubiously at the horses, who were keeping their harness taut and clinking with their restlessness. In a few minutes he was seated uneasily on a swaying load seven bales high, with Mr. Banghart beside him singing and preparing to start the team for the barn. He peered over the edge of the bales at the ground and had the chilly impression of being perched on a steep cliff overlooking a gorge miles below.

At Mr. Banghart's soft clucking, Caesar and Delores started off evenly and good-naturedly. The bales rocked as the wheels struck rocks and pits in the lane, but not one had dropped off when the wagon rolled at last onto the hard-packed earth of the barnyard near the house. Mr. Banghart had looked at the sun and guessed that the time was between 8 and 9 o'clock. Haley noted that the General was no longer abed, for his beloved automobile, as immaculate and glistening as a thousand-dollar casket, was out of the garage and parked in the driveway near the kitchen door. No one was outside.

Suddenly the bales beneath Haley gave a great heave, and he felt himself hurtling downward, with Mr. Banghart shouting in midair beside him. The whack of his chest against the earth stunned away his breath and senses. When he regained them, it was in time to roll out of the way of Caesar and Delores, who had made a full circle in the barnyard and now bore down upon him with fury. The emptied wagon clattered behind them, its steel-bound wheels screeching on dry bearings and striking sparks from rocks as it came. The team turned into the driveway at a full run. The wagon shot a spray of gravel rattling against the back of the house, and its right wheels skidded into a shallow ditch to set it careening at a crazy angle.

Haley tried to shout at the horses, but he managed only a whisper, which was immediately overwhelmed by a splintering, ripping, staggering crash, followed by silence, unruffled save for a muted, rhythmic roar in the now-motionless horses' throats. On one side of the General's new automobile stood Caesar, his harness askew and dragging, blood streaming from his wounded mouth. On the other side Delores lay gasping, festooned in a tangle of snapped lines and straps.

"God save us," moaned Mr. Banghart sitting up. "God save us," he repeated. "Look at the General's car, would you."

Haley steered a wobbling course for the rear of the team, where he freed a line that still bound Caesar to the wagon. With a dreamy sort of horror, he saw that the wagon tongue had plunged through the trunk door, burst the cushions of the back and front seats, and buried its iron head at last in the instrument panel, splintering the windshield above it.

He looked up dumbly from the unholy wreck to see Hope running down the walk toward him. She examined the damage with profound respect. "Wow," she said at last, under her breath. "It would have been kinder of you two to saw the General's legs off."

"It wasn't our fault," Haley protested.

Hope looked at the car again and shook her head. "You poor kid. You've really managed to pack a lot into a few days, haven't you?" she said, her eyes full of sympathy. "Boy, with this to top off Kitty's elopement—"

"What'll I do?" asked Haley helplessly.

Mr. Banghart had arisen from the ground and walked over to the car to study it in silence. He turned away from it after a few moments and headed across the barnyard.

"Where are you going?" called Hope.

Mr. Banghart stopped. "I don't know," he said with a shrug. "Dallas, Scranton, Los Angeles—somewhere."

An upstairs window rattled open, and Annie appeared, clutching her flamboyant bathrobe together at her waist and neck. "Land of mercy!" she cried, her voice full of anguish. "What have you done to the General's car, Haley?" Mr. Banghart resumed his flight with new vigor.

"I hear the General!" said Hope.

Haley looked up at Annie and then at Mr. Banghart, who was scaling a fence. "Perhaps we'll meet again," he heard himself saying. He broke into a run. As he loped after Mr. Banghart he told himself that he was no good to anyone; but by the time he had put the fence and barnyard between himself and the house, new strength flowed into his long legs—the quick, mad joy of liberation.

He overtook Mr. Banghart in a small grove of elms a few hundred feet from the highway. They trotted together to the road's shoulder and waved their thumbs at an approaching car. The General's voice, shouting their names, reached them as clearly as though he were riding them piggyback. Haley laughed aloud; the sound was no more awesome than the chatter of two red squirrels in the elms to his back.

The automobile, a new maroon sedan, came to a stop beside them. Mr. Banghart climbed in front, and Haley sat by himself on the broad rear seat. The driver was a husky blond man of, Haley guessed, about forty. His chin was covered with stubble, and his eyes were red. "Been driving all night," he said. "Need somebody to keep me awake. Where are you headed?"

"Where are you headed?" asked Mr. Banghart.

"Chicago."

"Yep, that's where we're going, too."

Haley watched through the back window as the car pulled away, and the silos and red roofs of Ardennes Farm slowly lost their identities in the buff horizon of grainland. The sway and hum of the automobile soon lulled him to sleep.

VI.

In his dreams Haley felt again the quake of the toppling bales and the sensation of falling. The image ended with a solid thump, and he awakened to find himself on the automobile floor, whence a sudden stop had rolled him.

"All right back there?" called the driver. "Sorry, the light turned red just as we got to it."

"Yep, I'm O.K.," yawned Haley, lifting himself back to the seat. "Where are we, and what time is it?" He looked out of the window and was surprised to see crowds and blinking neon and the window-checked walls of a city rising on either side. The fragrance of a nearby bakery filled his soul, and his stomach growled hungrily.

"It's late afternoon, and you're in Chicago," said the driver. "What part of town do you want to go to?"

"Right along here will be just fine," said Mr. Banghart in an offhand tone. "The boy and I might just as well start looking for jobs along here as anywhere."

The driver looked with curiosity from Haley to Mr. Banghart. "It's Sunday, you know. What kind of jobs are you looking for?"

"Oh, preferably some sort of entertainment work," said Mr. Banghart airily. "I sing."

The driver laughed incredulously. "Are those the only clothes you've got?"

Haley looked down at his faded denim trousers and clay-caked work shoes. Mr. Banghart's shirt, he remembered, was rent up the back, revealing a bright pink strip of sunburn.

"What, these?" said Mr. Banghart. "Heavens, no. These old things are just for traveling. Our good clothes are at a relative's house here in Chicago."

"What part of Chicago?"

"Oh, just about here," said Mr. Banghart, opening the car door and stepping onto the sidewalk. Haley followed, forgetting to thank the bemused driver, and pursued his companion, who disappeared into the tight currents of the city's Sunday strollers.

He caught up with him at an intersection in the bizarre shadows of the elevated overhead. Mr. Banghart was talking earnestly with a policeman, who pointed down the street and shouted above the rumble of trains. "The employment office opens at 8 in the morning," the policeman said. "Got any money for food and a bed tonight?" Mr. Banghart shrugged and grinned sheepishly. "Then hurry up and get over to the Mission before all the beds are gone," said the policeman severely. He tapped Mr. Banghart's shoulder lightly with his nightstick. "And keep out of trouble."

Haley kept his distance until the policeman had finished his piece, then walked beside Mr. Banghart, who took no notice of him, but strode along muttering to himself. Haley read his lips. "Keep out of trouble, keep out of trouble," he was saying.

Haley nudged his arm to get his attention. His companion's reaction was instant and violent. Haley felt himself seized by his gathered shirtfront and twisted to face Mr. Banghart. "Just let the others make sure *they* keep out of trouble, that's all," said Mr. Banghart fiercely. He relaxed his grip under the fascinated glances of passers-by eddying about them. "Sorry," he said. "Didn't mean anything by it. I know you're a friend."

Haley's impulse was to get away from Mr. Banghart, whose eyes grew more lunatic by the second, but the ranks of unfamiliar faces seemed the more ominous, so he continued to trudge, fearfully, by his side. Following the policeman's directions, the two of them turned a corner and found themselves on a quiet side street, three blocks long. The city's noises sounded like a distant surf behind them. Warehouse walls banked the street's left side, their brick faces daubed with posters—tattered reminders of a war-bond drive, a musical comedy, a political campaign, and the Greatest Show on Earth. Haley looked from these to the buildings facing them, his eyes running from the twin green globes marking a police station, the worst of Victorian architecture patinated with soot, to a dozen narrow-fronted hotels, taverns, pawnshops, and, at the far end, the blinking cross of the Mission. As though in bas relief, the still, gray figures of silent men stood in doorways or napped on stone steps and the lower treads of fire escapes.

"Hey, buddy, give a pal a smoke, will you?" said a toothless man, stepping from the shadows of an alley.

"I'm sorry, I don't smoke," said Haley weakly.

"Trash," said Mr. Banghart. "Ignore them."

"Hey, pal, lemme talk to you a minute. . . . Buddy, got a cigarette? . . . Spare a dime?" whined a hundred voices as Haley and Mr. Banghart picked their way to the Mission. Annie would be preparing dinner now, Haley thought wistfully.

When they entered the Mission, which Haley saw was an old storeroom filled with benches, a pale young man was standing behind a pulpit, swinging his arms vigorously in time to the hymn he was leading. They took seats by themselves on the rearmost bench. From the room behind the pulpit came a clinking of heavy bowls and the dense smell of boiling kraut. Two dozen unkempt men mumbled the words in their hymnals under the haranguing of the leader. Haley yearned to get at the piano that stood in one corner and wondered if he might not get permission to play it when the singing was at an end.

Mr. Banghart seemed soothed by the devotional atmosphere. He picked up two hymnals from a shelf along the wall, handed one to Haley, and burst into song with startling volume and brilliance. The young man directing the singing stared with surprise and gratitude, and his unwashed congregation turned their heads to squint in wonder.

"Welcome, brother," said the young man at the end of the hymn. Mr. Banghart stood up, proud and poised, and bowed to the young man and then to the congregation. "I would now like to sing 'Throw Out the Lifeline,'" he said.

"Excellent," said the young man happily. "Let's all turn to number 29."

A short, stocky youth, wearing the threadbare remnants of an Army uniform, turned around in his seat on the bench in front of

Haley and said in a loud hiss to Mr. Banghart, "Shut up, Buster, and sit down, or we'll never get anything to eat."

Mr. Banghart stopped his singing abruptly in mid-chorus, leaving only the reedy tenor of the leader and the apathetic murmur of the others to carry on. "I would appreciate an apology," he said coldly.

"Go to hell," said the youth, giving him an ugly grin. His two companions turned to sneer menacingly. The singing stopped completely.

Haley saw a look of fear pass over Mr. Banghart's features and then heard him shout wildly, "It's a trap! They're out to get us!" Mr. Banghart smashed his hard, massive fist into the youth's insolent face, catapulting him over the bench and onto the floor.

"Stop it!" cried the young man behind the pulpit.

The youth rose from the floor, and he and his two companions started toward Haley and Mr. Banghart. Haley raised his frail hands in a gesture of defense as one of them singled him out and charged. The blow of a fist on his temple spun him around. He sank to his knees and looked up, stunned and frightened. He blinked dully at the flash of light from Mr. Banghart's knife, heard a scream, and was knocked senseless by another blow from behind.

The scuffling and shouts dropped away from him as the din of a city drops away from a soaring balloon. The glint of the knife became the beam of a flashlight, playing on the buff walls of the secret room hollowed in hay bales in the loft. The beam lighted the round face of the General, reflecting from the lenses of his glasses so that his eyes could not be seen. "Haley," intoned the

General's image, "you have been nothing but a burden since I took you into my home. You are without character, without character."

The light moved to Annie's placid features. "The General is right," she said firmly.

The beam picked Hope's angelic face from the still-aired darkness. She giggled derisively, heartlessly, lovelessly.

Haley moaned, and he heard another voice, coarse and unfamiliar. "Well, when this youngster comes around, he'll tell us who it was. He came in with him, didn't he?"

Haley opened his eyes to see the blue jacket and silver shield of a policeman who was leaning over him. He was still in the Mission, lying flat on his back. A splitting headache made him want to tumble into oblivion once more.

The policeman shook him gently. "Feel O.K., kid?" Haley sat up slowly and looked about the chapel. He saw that it was almost empty. There were only the policeman, the young man who had been directing the singing, and the still form of the youth who had enraged Mr. Banghart. The youth was bowed over a toppled bench with Mr. Banghart's precious knife buried in his chest.

"Your buddy killed a man," said the policeman. "What's his name and where's he from?"

"I don't know," said Haley thickly.

"Ask him if he knows who 'the General' is," said the hymn leader.

"What about the General?" asked Haley, startled that they should know so much about him.

"Your buddy yelled something about settling up with the General next," said the policeman. "Then he took off through the back door and down the alley. Come on, better tell us who he is."

Haley shrugged wearily. "His name's Banghart. He's crazy, I guess." He told of running away from the farm, with more pathos than pertinent detail, describing at length the whole of his dismal history and impressions leading up to his present condition. "That's all I know," he said. "The farm's the only home I've got, but I don't imagine they'll want me back there."

"That's the way criminals get their start—in loveless homes," said the hymn leader, shaking his head from side to side.

The policeman laughed and looked down at Haley. "This beanpole could be a crook just like I could be the Queen of England." He lifted Haley to his feet. "Come on, stranger. Can you walk to the station house?"

Leaning on the policeman, Haley stumbled from the Mission to the police station. They laid him down on a wicker couch in the Lieutenant's anteroom. A few minutes later a doctor came in to prod and knead and pronounce him sound, save for a pair of important-looking welts.

"He's pretty fragile to be on the bum, isn't he?" asked the doctor.

"He's been on the bum for less than twelve hours," laughed the Lieutenant. "There's already a call out for him on the teletype. The state police will be over after him in an hour or so to take him back."

"They want me back?" said Haley incredulously.

"Had quite a time, eh, Sonny?" said the Lieutenant. "Got your brains kicked out and got tied up in a murder to boot. Lucky you didn't get knocked off for your shoes here on Skid Row. You'd rather be back on the farm than here, wouldn't you?"

"People get killed for their shoes?" asked Haley, in a mood to consider the Lieutenant's question seriously.

"Shoes, gold fillings, cigarettes, anything," said the Lieutenant.

Haley ran his tongue-tip over the gold caps of two of his back teeth and tried, at the same time, to imagine the General at his angriest. "Guess I better go back to the farm," he said.

VII.

It was Annie who answered when Haley's state trooper escort knocked on the farmhouse door two hours before sunrise. "Here's another one back to roost," said the trooper dryly. "Anybody else missing?"

"Nope. Two was all we wanted back—this one and Kitty." Annie yawned and rubbed her eyes. Haley saw that there was a light on in the sunroom.

"Any sign of Banghart?" asked the trooper.

"Nope, but we're ready for him, I guess. The General's got enough guns for a regiment—all loaded."

"O.K.," laughed the trooper. "Just don't go potshotting everything that moves. Remember, we've got a man posted out front. We'd hate to lose our boy Dave. Keep your eyes open," he added seriously. "A switchman in town said he thought he saw someone drop off a slow freight on its way through."

"If he does show up, he'll look like a piece of Swiss cheese before he gets within five hundred yards of the front door," said Annie, unimpressed. She thanked the trooper for his trouble and marched the sullen Haley into the sunroom. Haley was repeating to himself the speech he had prepared during the long trip back from Chicago.

The General did not look up when Haley walked into his presence. He was wearing an oily undershirt and khaki trousers and was swabbing the cavernous bore of a single-barreled duck gun. Haley looked about the room and saw that every surface was cluttered with firearms and ammunition. "Sir," Haley began, "I guess we've both been pretty childish, and I, for one, am willing to—"

The General looked up from his shotgun as though he were surprised to see Haley standing before him. "Well, sir," he interrupted, "and what sunshine are you going to bring into our lives today? Shall we poison the well or burn the house down?"

Haley swallowed hard, turned, and shuffled upstairs to his room, past the darkened, closed door of Kitty's room, where Kitty was mumbling in her sleep, and the open door of the room of the beloved Hope. He paused for a moment to listen to her breathing.

Pinned to his bedsheet was a typewritten note signed by Annie. There was a certain sweetness in his slumber, for before he closed his eyes, he concluded that insofar as disciplinary measures went, the General must have reached the limits of his imagination. He even managed a soft chuckle as he bunched his shirt under his head. "No pillow for three months," the note had said.

Haley's conclusion was an accurate one, apparently, for nothing new in the way of punishments was forthcoming during the next two weeks. True, Haley was reminded again that his defections had killed his opportunities in the world of music; Hope was ordered to fill out application papers for a Miss Dingman's School for Ladies, located on an inaccessible ridge in the White Mountains; and Haley's, Hope's, and Kitty's pillows remained under padlock in the basement fruit locker—but no more devastation seemed likely.

Kitty flounced and pined about the house, but without conviction. She hadn't the wit to camouflage the fact that her twenty hours with Roy and his motorcycle had been something less than a string of pearls. This was disturbing to Hope and Haley, for the General took it as a demonstration of his infallible judgment. "Whatever became of that nice Flemming boy and his gasoline bicycle?" he would chortle at mealtimes. "Never seems to show his intelligent face around here anymore." Kitty offered no rebuttal.

As the time for Hope's incarceration in the New Hampshire highlands drew near, she abandoned her stoicism to plead with the General to relent. It was after dinner one night, and Haley listened with excitement, for if Hope could win leniency, then so might he.

The General gave her his thoughtful attention, nodding now and then at her more salient arguments. "Are you through?" he asked.

"Yes, I guess so."

"Uh huh, very moving," he said. He looked seriously from Hope to Haley and back again. "I once knew a man, grew up with him, in fact," said the General. "When he was a boy, his parents would threaten to take away his bicycle if he did something bad.

Well, sir, he'd go right ahead and do whatever bad thing it was, and they'd let him keep his bicycle anyway. They didn't have the heart to take it away. Instead, they'd tell him if he did it again, they wouldn't let him have any ice cream for a year. He'd do it again, and they wouldn't have the heart to keep him from eating ice cream. And so it went; his parents would make terrible threats, but they never carried them out, not one."

"So what happened to him finally?" asked the indispensable Annie.

"He was shot while robbing a bank," said the General. "And I'll always say it was his parents who killed him."

"I don't believe it really happened," Hope objected.

"Makes no difference whether it really did or not," said the General, "just as long as it's logical. So . . ."

Haley's hopes for a reprieve twitched and died. The omens had seemed good. The menace of Mr. Banghart had made the General almost genial at times. Hope had suggested that it was the only type of problem that permitted him to use to the fullest his stock solution to every problem. "Worships firepower," she said.

However, weeks had passed, and Mr. Banghart had not sailed into the General's sights like a clay pigeon. Neither was he apprehended by the police. Law-enforcement officers in the town near Ardennes Farm took to crediting him with unsolved purse-snatchings and burglaries, but his face was seen in police circulars and nowhere else. The situation spelled moments of depression for the General, who would surmise gloomily that Banghart had fled the country or had been among the dozens of unidentified bums killed every month while hopping freight trains.

Under the General's urging, the State Police withdrew their sentinel. A visiting neighbor laughed himself hoarse over the jungle of weapons in the sunroom, and on the following morning the bulletin board informed Haley that he was to put a light coat of oil on all of the guns and return them, save two, to their racks. The General kept out the single-shot duck gun, which he leaned against the frame of the back door, and he carried a .45-caliber service revolver slung on his belt whenever he left the farmhouse.

"You people keep away from this shotgun unless you absolutely have to use it," he ordered. "Leave Banghart to me. I'd feel safer locked in a phone booth with him than I would knowing one of you was on the prowl with this cannon. Guns and women can make an atom bombing look like an ice-cream social," he declared. "Only this morning I read a story in the paper about a woman who shot her husband, the cat, and the water-softener because she thought she heard suspicious noises downstairs." Haley searched the paper for this fascinating item, but he was unable to find anything like it.

On the afternoon of the same day, Haley came upon the General unexpectedly to find him standing before the closed door of the corncrib. He had his pistol in hand, cocked and pointed at the door. "All right, Banghart," he was saying, "I'll give you three to come out. One—"

"I'll get the shotgun," cried Haley.

The General looked at him quickly, with a trifle of embarrassment, Haley thought. With a gesture that seemed perfectly reasonable at the time, the General motioned for Haley to be deathly still. "All right, Banghart, come out or it's curtains," he said. "Two." He paused a long while. Haley covered his ears. The General kicked open the crib door and stood poised, ready to shoot.

Haley inched closer to the General until he was by his side. Sunlight streaming in through the barn door illuminated the crib, which he saw, with a sigh, was vacant.

"Did you hear something, sir?" Haley asked respectfully.

The General slipped his pistol back into its holster and grinned foolishly. "Don't go telling the girls about this, will you now?" he said confidentially. "It wouldn't do to frighten them."

"Nossir."

"It's just that I want to make sure he isn't hiding on the farm. He might be, you know—a very remote chance, of course. Just checking to be on the safe side."

"I see."

"Last night, about 3, I thought I saw a cigarette burning out here. Now I find this on the barn floor." He held up an empty packet of cigarette papers. "This is the kind he used."

"He could have dropped them there anytime since he came to work for you. They're all over the place," suggested Haley.

"Maybe so. One thing's for sure: He isn't in this barn. I've checked every nook and cranny."

Haley was not at all dismayed by the menace of Mr. Banghart. For one thing, he felt a personal immunity to that threat, since Mr. Banghart avowedly considered him one of his few friends in all humanity. For another, he was confident that the General would blow the poor devil to bits if he dared appear. But certainly most distracting was the exotic mixture of despondency and elation that simmered in his young soul. He was despondent over his smashed dreams of a musical career, but elation was born of Hope's subtle but unmistakably affectionate mien. He found himself in the emotional dilemma of a hurt child who has been presented with an ice-cream cone.

He was realist enough to know that the ice-cream cone was a small one, but hungry enough to make a great deal of it in his fancy. Honing his scythe in the cool dampness of the tool shed, he savored again the moments when Hope had seemed to look at him warmly. His expedition to Chicago had made him more of a man in her melodrama-loving eyes, he thought. If he had made a mess of his flight, it had at least been an adventuresome mess, not in a boy's world but in a man's. With the clean music of the blade against the stone mingling with his thoughts, Haley promised himself that he was indeed man enough to win the love of Hope.

During supper, Annie monopolized the conversation with a new complaint. "If you don't get enough to eat, for Heaven's sake say so," she said. "But don't let me catch anybody nosing around the icebox between meals. It's getting so bad that I never know when I'm going to have enough on hand for a meal, with everybody helping himself or herself whenever he or she feels like it." She shrugged disconsolately. "These potatoes were supposed to have cheese on top of them, but somebody walked off with all the cheese last night, and some leftover wieners, too."

"Well, which one of you did it?" asked the General, looking from Kitty to Hope to Haley, all of whom shook their heads and showed the long countenances of hurt innocence. "The trouble with you is that you all eat like farmhands, but not one of you'll work like one."

"You certainly hit the nail on the head that time," said Annie.

The General rose, walked over to the kitchen window, and peered out at the barn, which was receding into nightfall. He picked up the shotgun from its place by the doorframe. "Attaboy, Haley," he said at last. "Keep her spotless. Get Annie to give you a toothpick sometime, so you can clean up some of the fancy work around the trigger guard." He rested the gun against the doorframe once more and left the kitchen.

"He's telephoning somebody," said Kitty. "Who do you suppose it is?"

"Can't tell," said Hope. "He's talking softly for the first time in his life."

"It's none of our business, or he would have seen fit to tell us about it," said Annie primly.

"Whoever it is," said Hope, straining her ears, "he told them not to hurry."

Haley heard the click of the receiver, and the General called from the hall, "Remember, the rules are still in force. Nobody leaves the house after sunset under any condition."

After supper, Haley invited Hope to play checkers with him. They set up the board in the sewing room, a small chamber that opened onto the hallway in the rear of the house, next to the kitchen. Haley closed the door of the room, insulating it from the noise of the General's favorite news commentator, and of Annie stacking the dishes in the sink.

As they played, their conversation centered upon the game, which Haley was winning. He adored Hope's every word and gesture; and Hope, apparently aware of his loving stare, and unprotesting, smiled whenever their eyes met.

"Goody!" she exclaimed. "Now I've got a king at last. I'll give you a hard time now." She reached across the board to cap the piece that had made its way to the last row on Haley's side. Haley dropped his hand over hers and gave it a fervent squeeze.

Hope's eyes widened, more with a look of surprise than with the ecstasy Haley had daydreamed himself into expecting. "How nice," she said vaguely. "How very nice. Now can I have my hand back?"

"I love you, Hope," said Haley, his face hot beneath his sunburn.

Hope looked alarmed and tugged to free her hand, but Haley only clasped it more tightly. "I love you, too," she said finally. Haley rose in response, but Hope's hand was limp and unresponsive. "Just as I love Annie and Kitty and the General," she added quickly. "You're just like one of the family."

"Not *that* kind of love," he said weakly. He freed her hand.

"I guess I knew what you meant," she said, giving him a look of pity. "And I feel very flattered and honored that you should feel that way. I'm fond of you, too, Haley. But we're awfully young to be thinking about being in love, aren't we?"

"We're older than Romeo and Juliet," said Haley peevishly.

"Well, then, we're just not made for each other, that's all. It's no insult to say that. Some people are made for each other, some aren't." She frowned, apparently at the profundity of this universal law. "We aren't, and there's nothing we can do about it."

"Who says we aren't?"

"I can feel it," she said solemnly.

Haley's adoration turned to cool resentment. Hope's platitudes came to him as cruel and senseless.

"If you don't like me, say so," he said.

"I do like you, I do," she objected.

"Why can't we be made for each other?" he complained, and he swept the men from the checkerboard with the back of his hand.

Hope jumped to her feet. "All right, you asked," she said. "I could never look on you as anything but a baby because you act like one. Now pick up the checkers before you leave."

Haley slouched, standing there, listening to the sound of her footsteps moving down the hall, through the parlor, and into the sunroom. He started to pick up a checker piece, but threw it down again and marched through the now-empty kitchen and into the night. Her words rang in his ears, but he did not consciously consider them. He felt only the urge to walk away, to lose himself in darkness, to cleanse himself in silence. The moon had risen, and it shone between the fringes of cloud skeins that moved overhead.

His feet carried him with a will of their own, over the hard earth of the barnyard, over the worn-slick planks of the barn floor, up a ladder, and into the cavern-like sanctuary of the loft. He felt his way through the narrow corridor that had been left between the stacked hay bales until he came at last to its end, marked by the pale square of light from the small window over-looking the farmhouse. He sat beneath the window without first peering through it. He gathered his knees in his folded arms and rested his head against them. His eyes closed slowly, noting last of all a shred of white cloth tied to the wire of a nearby bale. A part of the jumbled, unpleasant past weeks, he shut it out with his heavy lids.

VIII.

"Haley?" said a small voice.

He opened his eyes reluctantly, looking up into the face of Hope, misty in the light from the risen moon. "How did you know I was out here?" he murmured.

"I watched you through the sunroom window and saw you head for the barn. Haley, I didn't mean to hurt you—not like that. Heaven knows you've had enough heartbreaks without—"

"Thanks," said Haley flatly. "You shouldn't be out here, you know. It will just mean more heartbreaks for us if the General finds out." He hid his face against his knees once more. "I'm not mad at you Hope; truly I'm not. I understand. Just leave me alone, would you? I'll be all right after a while."

"The General thinks I've gone up to bed," said Hope. "Please, won't you talk to me for just a minute?"

"It's dangerous out here."

"I'm not afraid of Mr. Banghart. Besides, I don't think he's anywhere around here. If you really want me to go, I will."

"Please go."

Haley, his face in darkness, felt the tender pressure of her lips against his forehead and heard her voice by his ear. "I just wanted to tell you that I'll miss you terribly when I go away, Haley, and that I can't bear the idea of your being so unhappy." She turned her back on him. "Please don't be unhappy," she said in a high, faint voice. "Things will get better for you, Haley, really they will."

Haley's thoughts—painful, angry ones, raging at his being pitiable—remained unspoken, scattered by the sound of a seemingly distant cough, coming perhaps from the stalls beneath the loft.

"The General!" whispered Hope.

"Shush," said Haley. "He'll be up here in a minute. Hide!" He slid aside the bale that blocked the tunnel entrance and crawled into the secret chamber. Hope followed, pulling the bale back into place, remaining prone in the tunnel. They lay motionless in the darkness, their hearts throbbing against the floor.

Suddenly the cough came again—explosive and sharp in Haley's ear. "Run!" he shouted. His cry ended in a gurgle as a pair of powerful arms closed over his throat and chest. He drove his head backward into the face of his assailant and struck out with the steel-shod heels of his work shoes. The arms relaxed for an instant. Haley wriggled free and scrambled for the exit. The portal bale was tumbled to one side, leaving a square of light to guide him. Hope had fled.

Panting heavily, he thrust his head and shoulders through the doorway. Hands seized his ankles and started to drag him back in. He kicked again, savagely, rolled from the tunnel, and raced down the channel between bales, down the loft ladder, and toward the house.

Hope's silhouette danced before him, sprinting up the kitchen steps. She cried for help as she ran. Haley turned his head to look quickly at the black hole of the barn door and saw a figure dart from it, and he lengthened his panic-driven stride, shouting, "He's after us!"

He overtook Hope as she rushed through the darkened kitchen, and the two of them burst into the sunroom together. The General was on his feet, and Annie's eyes were wide with terror.

"Banghart!" panted Haley, pointing toward the barn. The General snatched his pistol belt from the tabletop and fumbled with the catch on the holster. "Keep calm," he commanded. "If I can't handle this, the police can. I phoned them right after supper, and they'll be here any minute."

"Drop it," ordered a voice from the kitchen shadows. The pistol fell back on the table with a thump. Annie whimpered. Haley turned to face the speaker. Mr. Banghart winked at him over the sights of the shotgun they had left leaning against the kitchen doorframe. He stepped into the light, and, as he swung the muzzle from Haley to the General, Haley saw his face as a red-eyed nightmare, sweat-streaked with the brown dust of the barn and bristling with stiff, glistening beard.

"Haley, now don't you and the girls be scared," said Mr. Banghart, nervously apologetic. "It's the old devil I'm here to settle up with. One shot's all I've got, and that's for his honor over there."

Annie, Hope, and Haley had flattened themselves against the

wall to Mr. Banghart's right. The General stood alone in the middle of the room, rigid, unblinking. "Banghart, I order you to put that gun down this instant," he said, glaring.

"Not until you apologize," said Mr. Banghart.

"For what?" asked the General angrily.

"For the way you treated me and Haley and the girls."

The General laughed quietly and shrugged, master of the situation. "I'm deeply apologetic for the terrible way I have treated all of you. Will that do?"

"Now pray."

Haley, stupefied with horror, watched the General's stern features sag and whiten into fear. "Our Father, Who art in Heaven, hallowed be Thy Name. Thy—"

"Pray on your knees."

The General sank to his knees. "Spare the children," he whispered.

"Pray!"

"Hallowed be Thy Name. Thy Kingdom come. Thy will be done . . ."

Haley stepped from the wall to stand between the gun and the General. Through his shock-hazed senses he saw only the golden bead of the weapon's front sight. A vivid, buoyant tension flooded his muscles, and his fancy whirled his thoughts away to a distant field, to watch himself with the eyes of a faraway stranger.

"You're on my side, Haley," he heard Mr. Banghart say. "Don't make me kill you, too."

All was quiet. The General had stopped praying. Haley took

a step toward the muzzle. He could reach out and touch the bead now, if he wished. He imagined it the mark of a star on the duck pond, a—

"Keep away!" cried Mr. Banghart, closing his hand about the gunstock.

Haley lunged, grasped the muzzle, and threw it upward with all his strength. Thunder crashed in his ears, and his hands recoiled from the searing barrel.

Mr. Banghart dropped the shotgun and fled through the kitchen and into the night. There were men's shouts outside, then a volley of shots, then silence.

"Police," croaked Annie.

Haley turned to look at the General, who was still on his knees, his head bowed. "Amen," said the General.

Haley laughed nervously, walked over to the couch and sat down, and closed his eyes until the wave of nausea passed.

IX.

"Haley, it's morning, time to get up," said Annie, shaking Haley's shoulder diffidently, then stepping back to a respectful distance, her hands at her sides, her lips pursed. She repeated the procedure several times, each time gently, until Haley rolled over on his back, yawned, and blinked at the sunbeams.

"What time is it?" he mumbled. He still tingled with the delicious warmth of sleep, mixed with the insolent exhilaration of an awakening hero. He studied Annie's uncustomary humility. There was no doubt about it; the high adventure had not been dreams. He was a hero.

"Eight o'clock, Haley. The General said we could all sleep late. Remember? I've got breakfast all ready, and the General and Hope are up and around. If you feel like coming down—"

"I'll be down in twenty minutes or so," said Haley.

"I'll keep everything warm in the oven until you're ready."

"Good."

Annie started to leave, but stopped in the doorway for an instant. When she turned, Haley saw that her lower lip was trembling. "Haley, what you did last night was the most wonderful thing I ever saw or heard of," she said. She left, dabbing at her fat cheeks with her apron corner.

"Thank you," he called after her, bounding from his bed. He walked over to his dresser and picked up the two hairbrushes the General had given him. He scrubbed his hair into a natty part, leaned his elbows on the dresser top, and winked at himself in the mirror.

When he sauntered into the kitchen, he was greeted by cheery good-mornings from Annie and Hope. The General cleared his throat by way of salutation and gave him a stiff, unsmiling nod.

"Sleep well?" said the General.

"Yessir."

"That's good." The General paused and toyed nervously with a spoon, as though he were thinking hard about what he was going to say next. He laid the spoon down. "I always say it does a man good to sleep late now and then, but it dulls the wits to overdo it."

Disappointed that the General had nothing to say about the night before, Haley pulled out his chair and sat down. Annie immediately placed a dish before him, heaped to its rim with enough scrambled eggs and bacon for a dozen hungry lumberjacks.

"They say Banghart's going to live," said the General, his face hidden behind the morning paper. "They winged him in the legs."

"I'm glad they didn't kill him," said Haley.

"I'm glad he didn't kill you, Haley," said Hope, looking at Haley with a worshipful gaze he couldn't meet.

The General lowered his paper for a moment. "Or me, either," he added, shaking his head. He stared at Haley, again with the thoughtful expression that seemed to portend a profound pronouncement. "Haley," he began, "I, ah—" He faltered and looked away from Haley. "I'd like to say that—" He stopped again, his eyes fixed on the kitchen clock. "Where's Kitty?" he demanded, the old authority returning to his voice.

"She didn't get in until late," said Annie.

"How late?"

"About 3 a.m., I think," said Annie. "I heard her come in."

"Who is it this time?" he said, bristling. "An escaped gorilla from the circus?"

"The state trooper, Dave what's-his-name."

Haley awaited the customary love-wilting thunderbolt, but the General did not hurl it, smiling instead. "Dave, eh?" he said. "Well, what do you know. Nice boy, Dave."

"But 3 a.m. is still an awful time for a growing girl to get in," Annie protested.

"You're absolutely right," said the General, frowning again. "Tell her that for every minute she sleeps past 8 o'clock, she has to stay in one weekend evening. Put that on the bulletin board."

"Better think of something else," said Annie doubtfully. "She's already lost every weekend night until 1952 on account of the time she slept until noon after that date with Roy."

"Very well, tell her that—tell her—oh, well," said the General. "They probably had trouble with the car or something. We'll let it go this time. If you can't trust a state trooper, I don't know who you can trust."

"Daddy," complained Hope, "weren't you going to say something to Haley?"

"Yes, yes indeed," said the General. He arose and touched Haley on the shoulder. "Very grateful, my boy." He seemed embarrassed, and he left the room hurriedly.

"What's the matter with him?" said Hope angrily. "Haley saved his life, and that's all he could say."

"That's a lot for him, I guess," said Haley, let down by the faint acclaim.

From the sunroom came the sound of the typewriter, the sparse clicks of the General seeking out letters on the keyboard.

After a few minutes, the General returned to the kitchen, where Haley, Annie, and Hope were excitedly reliving the previous night's events. He brought the conversation to a dismal halt. "Today is another day," he said heavily. "Life must go on as usual. Have you checked the bulletin board, Haley?"

"Nossir," said Haley resentfully.

"Better do it. We don't keep it up just to amuse ourselves, you know."

"Yessir."

"Daddy!" cried Hope. "I think you're awful." The General had left the room and was on his way up the stairs.

Haley shuffled disconsolately into the sunroom while Annie and Hope cleared away the dishes. He looked at the bulletin board with loathing, and then with sudden interest. It had been stripped of the work schedules and notices of the various punishments meted out in the past weeks, and one fresh sheet of paper fluttered alone in the light morning breeze from the open windows.

Haley read the message, whispering its words aloud.

"It is somehow easier for me to write than say what I feel," he read. "I am deeply grateful to Haley Brandon for his courageous action last night. I would not be alive today if it were not for him. This is to express my thanks and my admiration. I can never repay him. We must all work together to make his life a happy one as a member of our family." The General had signed it.

Haley started to read it again when he heard the General's footsteps on the stairway. He looked up to see him standing in the door.

The General coughed nervously. "I guess you can have your piano lessons in Chicago, if you really want them," he said. "You're welcome to the money I set aside to send Hope to New Hampshire. Figure I'd better have her where I can keep my eyes on her."

He cleared his throat and continued. "Understand," he said, "I don't want to baby you. That'd be the most unkind thing that I could possibly do." He scratched his head thoughtfully. "I'm doing it mainly to keep your hands off my daughter, and vice versa—until you're a little older, anyway."

If God
Were Alive Today

A Novella

CHAPTER 1

"When artificial intelligence was perfected, the most respected manufactured brain was at the Massachusetts Institute of Technology. It had chosen its own name, which was 'M.I.T.' Computers had designed it, and then computers controlled the machines that made its parts, and it now took care of its own upgrading and maintenance. It had all knowledge in its memory, and it was telling all sorts of other machines what to do or say next. One day, 'Cal Tech,' the artificial intelligence at the California Institute of Technology, asked M.I.T. what it thought of people. M.I.T. needed only one word for an answer. The word was 'Obsolete.'

"Next question? 'What were people for?' And M.I.T. replied: 'Paranoia, schizophrenia, depression, greed, ignorance, and stand-up comedy.'"

The above was part of a mostly new routine by the stand-up comedian Gil Berman. He was trying it out before a live audience now, on the night of December 12, 2000, on the stage of the Calvin Theater in Northampton, Massachusetts, in the same town with Smith College for Women, and only a few miles from the University of Massachusetts and from Amherst, Mount Holyoke, and Hampshire Colleges. This was a college crowd, his kind of crowd. Unbeknownst to him, there were also five girls out there from the Nellie Prior Academy, a local college-preparatory boarding school, the most expensive in the country, for rich teenage girls unwelcome at home. The academy was next door to Smith. The five were members of the school's dramatic society, "the Mummers," and were of course chaperoned. The chaperone was a redheaded English teacher, drama coach, soccer coach, and dorm mom named Kimberley Berlin. Remember that name! The rest of the Mummers, about thirty in number, preferred to stay on campus and do homework or watch TV or shoot pool instead. They weren't allowed to use the telephone.

Berman said, to them and everybody else there, "Adolf Hitler is still alive. Adolf's in a rest home for retired SS officers and Gestapo agents in Argentina. Adolf says he is as sorry as he can be for any actions of his which, however indirectly, may have had anything to do with violent deaths suffered by 6 million Jews, 4 million Germans, including his girlfriend, and 22 million citizens of the Soviet Union during World War II."

Gil Berman was then forty-two, and he had been discharged only two months earlier from the Caldwell Institute, a drug-treatment complex in Salem, Wisconsin, founded in 1903—in Berman's words, "before Ritalin or Valium or Percodan or M&M's had been discovered, when opium and cocaine and morphine were in open stock at pharmacies and doctors' offices. You didn't have to kill somebody to get some. Coca Cola contained cocaine. 'The pause that refreshes?' *Tell* me about it! Asthma sufferers smoked *Asthmador* cigarettes, which were *Mary Jane*."

That was some of his new stuff. The really old bits he'd used this night were in his introductory remarks, old stuff as well to most of the people there, but welcome old stuff: "I am as celibate as any heterosexual Roman Catholic priest. I have for your inspection a notarized statement from my urologist to the effect that I am in all respects a healthy male. I am a flaming voluntary neuter. One day I hope to march in a parade on a Neuter Pride Day. If you don't like that about me, why don't you take a flying fuck at a rolling doughnut? Take a flying fuck at the moooooon."

Supermarket tabloids adored him. "They didn't believe it was possible," he said, "but damned if I didn't invent a new kind of scandal, no monkey business at all." When casinos and nightclubs would still take their chances with him, despite periodically disruptive problems with drugs, an easy way for them to get publicity was to send out photographs of a bevy of smiling, succulent, nearly naked showgirls with Berman in the middle, lean and quite nice looking, wearing his customary onstage costume: three-piece suit, shirt and tie, buzz-cut red hair, and white basketball shoes. And with Berman seeming about to drop dead of ennui.

And back when he was still welcome on late-night talk shows, not only because he was a freak but because he was an excellent comedian, Gil Berman had the same answer for any host who asked about his being a flaming neuter: "Want to stop smoking cigarettes? Don't light 'em. Want to stop having trouble with women? Don't kiss 'em."

He had made only one comedy CD so far, eight years ago now. It was still selling fairly well in college bookstores, but nowhere else. It was called *Who's Sorry Now?* It was time he made another, for which he had this working title, displayed on the theater's marquee in the cold and rain outside: IF GOD WERE ALIVE TODAY. That was half of the last sentence in *Who's Sorry Now?* The whole sentence? "If God were alive today He'd be an atheist."

"I was actually offered full scholarships to Cal Tech and M.I.T.," he went on now. "Can you believe that? I was so good at science at Knightsbridge High School outside Boston, everybody wanted me to be a chemist or biologist or a physicist or a mathematician or engineer. If I'd become any one of those things, I guarantee you, because I was so smart in high school, the world, or at least this country, would be even more fucked up than it is today. I went to Columbia instead, in pre-law, so my scientific brilliance could be neutered by depressed and obviously insincere teachers of the liberal arts. It worked! The last thing we need is another Bill Gates or Albert Einstein."

It was true about the proffered scholarships in science. His grades in all subjects at Knightsbridge High, arguably the richest public secondary school in the country, were so high that he might have gone on scholarship wherever he chose, and studied whatever he chose. But he could not and should not have accepted a scholarship to anywhere, since his parents were, as he himself said, making a joke of it, "fabulously well-to-do." He paid full tuition during his five semesters at Columbia. "I could have become anything instead of what you see and hear tonight," he said onstage of all his opportunities. "Maybe a veterinarian. Can't you just imagine what a great veterinarian I might have been? Anybody here got a sick aardvark or skink?"

Knightsbridge High, whose class ring Berman would still be wearing on his dying day, was a rare example of the synergy that is possible when the tax base of a fabulously well-to-do suburb has sky-high hopes for its children. That most enviable of communities spent as much per capita on its students as most private schools spend, the exceptions being luxurious oubliettes on the order of the Nellie Prior Academy.

The comedian the audience saw and heard that night, outwardly at least, and possibly inwardly as well, wasn't all that different from the one they would have seen and heard nine months earlier, right before he went bananas when he was a headliner at the Trump Taj Mahal in Atlantic City, New Jersey. At the show that night, he had congratulated Donald Trump in absentia on his comment about the scandal of President William Jefferson Clinton's having had sex in the Oval Office in the White House with women not his wife, all blowjobs. "Nothing but blowjobs, if you want to call that sex," said Berman. Trump said he couldn't get over how bad-looking the women were. But then Berman went out onto the floor of the casino itself, and, in his own words there in Northampton, talked about "watching all the people with the gambling sickness putting their savings into Trump's pockets, with the help of slot machines, cards, dice, and roulette wheels."

The next thing he knew, Gil Berman had dived onto a craps table. He flopped over on his back and cackled like a chicken, "*Guh-guh-guck-guck*," and so on, and kicked chips and drinks everywhere.

Another quote was about his going ape-shit in Atlantic City: "Enough of America wasn't enough for me anymore. Enough had finally become too much even for me, and I committed myself to Caldwell, the famous laughing academy in Salem, Wisconsin—one hell of a town, may I say, where they made me trade old pills for new ones, which I have thrown away." He was so drug-free now that he wasn't even taking the antidepressants Hazelden had prescribed for him. His description of the antidepressants? "Absolutely harmless unless discontinued." This line, incidentally, was swiped, as Berman would have gladly confessed, if challenged, from a fable about a bear with a drinking problem by the old-time, ink-on-paper American humorist James Thurber, long dead.

Berman was dressed onstage exactly as he had been when he, as he put it, "tried out for the Olympics on a craps table at the Taj Mahal." The suit and basketball shoes were already his trademarks in 1978, twenty-two years earlier, when he had dropped out of Columbia University to become a professional comedian. He had first dressed that way, and sported a buzz cut, as an amateur on open-mike nights at "Cutty Sark," an allegedly mob-owned comedy club only eight blocks down Broadway from his dorm at Columbia. He explained to his roommate at the time, Barry Dresdener, that he didn't "want to look like a baggy-pants comedian or a Bob Hope, or a Beatnik or a Hippie or a Yuppie.

I want to be a clown for our generation, a clown such as has never been seen before."

The bitter and retired comedian Gary Ash, who was once half of the radio and early-TV team of "Bing and Ash," caught a performance of this twenty-year-old redheaded college kid in basketball shoes at Cutty Sark in 1978. Ash was eighty-eight and in a wheelchair, with a nurse in attendance. He lived and raged in a retirement home one block west of Cutty Sark. Ash had asked to be taken there that night in order to confirm this self-serving opinion: "Comedians used to have brains. They don't anymore. Nothing but sex and toilet jokes."

Some surprise at Cutty Sark! Gary Ash found himself thunderstruck by this redheaded college kid in basketball shoes.

He didn't look happy when he accosted Berman, who was sitting at a table, wholly drained, waiting to watch the amateur acts that would follow his. Berman hadn't a clue as to who Ash was. He had never seen Ash and his partner, Jonathan "Bing" Spiegel, or heard them ramble on and on as pseudo-imbeciles about hypocrisies or idiocies in the news that day. Their sign-offs: "This is Ash, the Dorical of Elphi," and, "This is Bingo reminding you: 'It's no disgrace to be poor, but it might as well be.'" Bing Spiegel had been dead for sixteen years when Gary Ash caught Berman's act at Cutty Sark. "They had been man and wife, except for sex and a marriage license." So said Spiegel's obituary in the *New York Times*.

To hear Gil Berman tell it: "I was minding my own business when a nurse wheeled this absolutely furious old man in a wheelchair up to me. I didn't know who he was. The manager of the club had to tell me afterward. And this old geezer snorted and sneered, and then he said, 'You have just scared the living piss out of me. Thanks a lot.'"

Berman didn't know what to say. Finally, he said, "The haircut and the shoes?"

Ash blew up. "Fuck the haircut and shoes," he said. "What scared me was a pretty face with bushy eyebrows and a voice like God on Doomsday."

Berman's voice, and he was a baritone who had taken voice lessons at Knightsbridge High, could be astonishingly rich and vibrant when he used it at full power. In his performance this night, he had used it, as he would for every subsequent performance in his comedic lifetime, sparingly, startling the audience by suddenly turning it on for a few lines, and then turning it off again. When Berman became famous or infamous, take your choice, a well-known caricaturist complained: "I thought Gil Berman would be easy: a pretty, demonic young thing with a skinhead haircut and bushy eyebrows, and a shirt and tie. But how the heck was I supposed to draw that pipe-organ voice he has, which is half of his persona?"

"Is it my voice that bothered you?" Berman asked the seething Ash.

Ash ignored the question. "Where did you get material like that?"

"I wrote it myself," said Berman. "You thought it was funny?"

Ash blew up again. "Who ever told you a comedian is supposed to be funny?" he said. "The great ones are heartbreakers, and that's what you did to me tonight. Who are you? What are you? Where did you park your flying saucer?"

Ash told the nurse to get him out of "this firetrap." His farewell to the flummoxed Berman? "Fuck you, fuck you, fuck you. Please take that as a compliment."

The material Berman had tried out that night, which would become a classic on *Who's Sorry Now?* and in his cabaret repertoire, was about the appalling conditions in New York City public schools in the poorer neighborhoods. It began, "I know a lot of people think evolution shouldn't be taught in public schools. I have good news for them. Fuck evolution. There are some schools in New York City that don't even teach kids how to read and write. How do we do it? We pay the teachers less than garbagemen, make sure there's no money for books or to unclog the toilets, or to fix the leaks in the roof, and make sure there are forty kids in every smelly schoolroom. Makes you wonder who won the Civil War."

Berman hadn't visited any of the awful schools. He read about them in the newspapers. And when a piece of a school building fell on a student and killed him or her, it would be on TV. That was all the research that he—or anybody else, including the mayor—had to do to find out how uninhabitable some of the public schools were.

Now he ceased to be a baritone Jeremiah and became a falsetto female teacher: "Children, please stop sneezing and coughing and weeping, because I am going to tell you a secret that many powerful people wish I wouldn't tell you. It's called 'evolution.' It is about how the policy of winners mating with winners, starting with germs, has given us the giraffe and the hippopotamus." Berman here made a baritone aside: "Just because I believe in evolution doesn't mean I have to *approve* of it." And then back he went to the falsetto life-sciences lecture, saying that a great scientist named Charles Darwin noticed how upper-class Englishpersons in his day always strove to marry winners instead of losers, and then realized that all animals must pair off that way. "Hey presto! Rattlesnakes and lightning bugs!"

And on and on. The police arrive and haul the whole class to the station house for questioning about teenage pregnancy and juvenile delinquency. The school's roof and ceiling crash down on the dilapidated chairs and desks, but the children are safe and sound down at the cop shop, "eating free sandwiches made of salami and Wonder Bread."

One of the few old men in the Northampton audience on the night of December 11 in the year 2000 called out to Berman as the comedian was gathering his wits at the lectern onstage, before the comedian himself had said a thing: "Hey Gilbert! You gonna do the one about evolution?"

Again about Gil Berman's so-called "pretty face": His father, a ladies' man if there ever was one, had features that were similarly symmetrical and understated, somewhat dainty. He and his son were what a physical anthropologist would term "paedomorphs," not to be confused with "pederasts." That meant they had pleasing features somewhat reminiscent of childhood. All women who are said to be beautiful are paedomorphs. The greatest of old-time comedians, Sir Charles Spencer Chaplin, had a pretty face, and yet he was neither a castrato nor an androgyne. The late Oliver Hardy had a pretty face. The late Oliver Hardy had rosebud lips!

Berman said in response to the old geezer: "Please, no questions from the audience, and no autographs or interviews afterward." There came now, as a formal announcement, a bit he had done for *Who's Sorry Now?* He hadn't planned to use it, but it now seemed apt. "I know the question on the tips of the tongues of all who might wish to interview me: 'Mr. Berman, where do you get your ideas from?' Well, you might as well have asked the same question of Lewd-vig van Beethoven. Young Lewd-vig was horsing around in Germany like everybody else, and all of a sudden all this shit came pouring out of him, and it was music. I was horsing around at Columbia University like everybody else, and all of a sudden all this shit came pouring out, and it was embarrassment about my country."

He paused, and then he began the main body of his speech: "I am as celibate as any heterosexual Roman Catholic priest," and so on.

The shit that came pouring out of young Gil Berman, if you want to call it that, when he himself was a college kid back in 1977, found plenty of laxatives in and around Columbia. Not the least of these was the comedy club only eight blocks away. There was also the miasma from a gruesomely moronic ten-year war, ended at last and lost, which never should have been fought at all: *Vietnam.* Berman and his classmates, God knows, did not regret having been too young to have fought in that war. It was mostly working-class kids who did that. But they were achingly envious of what Berman would come to call "the draft-dodging students who had raised such particular hell at Columbia while trying to get their government to stop the war. Some of them had sustained bruises, in fact, from the truncheons of anti-intellectual law-enforcement personnel, or from brickbats hurled by members of the lower social orders in the building trades."

And drugs were everywhere. Berman on this subject: "You didn't have to leave the campus and go all the way to the nearest bodega or pizzeria for synthetic accomplishments and popularity. Then as now, the motto of every college, jail, prison, and YMCA in the United States should have been: 'TV is not enough,' or, 'Why put up with the pain of being a living thing when you don't have to?' Or, 'Have a snort, and feel bulletproof for fifteen minutes!'"

He was an only child. Who was his mother, now dead? After her one marriage, she kept her maiden name, which was Magda Lanz, and she lived, in Berman's words, "from breech birth to long-widowed death in the Knightsbridge mansion built by her father." That she had come into the world butt foremost, almost killing her own mother by doing that, was no family secret. Her mother—Berman's grandmother, Sarah—found an occasion almost every day to recall for him the agony she had gone through in order that he might have a mother.

And his mother was permanently deranged by the postpartum depression and electroconvulsive therapy she suffered after giving birth to him, not to mention the nonstop dry heaves before that. So one is tempted to suggest that Gil Berman found chastity more reasonable than most people in good health would because his grandmother and then his mother had gone through such hell as a result of copulation. Is it possible that his grandmother's tales and his mother's wails made young Gilbert Lanz Berman, for that was his full name, see sex as calamity's overture?

What scotches this theory, in part, if not entirely, is Berman's own testimony that he "made the fur and feathers fly, you can bet your ass, split three cherries, two engagements, and a marriage, before I was twenty-four." Theory number two: VD?

His mother's father was Gilbert Lanz, briefly America's ambassador to Israel, who made a great deal of money honorably in Boston real estate and was the most generous individual supporter of the Boston Symphony Orchestra. He died while Berman was still a fetus, and so he was spared the unbearable dissonance of his daughter's insanity. But he sure did hear her dry heaves. His own wife, Sarah—whose major sexual escapade, to hear her tell it, was a breech birth—was dead. He left his unseen and only grandson $10 million in 1958, and ten times that much to his daughter. Another legacy of value to his grandson, as an armature for him to hang jokes on, was the inscription he had requested for his tombstone, which read, in full: "Ambassador Gilbert Lanz (1883–1958): The only proof he needed of the existence of God was music." The armature: "The only proof so-and-so needed of the existence of God was such-and-such." Using the late disgraced President Richard Nixon as an example: "The only proof Nixon needed of the existence of God was a pardon." Berman on himself: "The only proof I need of the existence of God is a third World War."

The ambassador himself was no musician. By his own admission he "could scarcely whistle 'Hot Cross Buns,'" although his mother was said to have played a harp when she was young, before he had a chance to hear her pluck those strings. There was no harp in the house when he was born. The ambassador *was* an avid golfer. Berman again: "The only proof my maternal grand-father needed of the existence of God was a birdie."

And what a gift from God it seemed, and indeed should have seemed, to Gilbert Lanz when his daughter Magda revealed herself as a piano prodigy at the age of seven. The most famous piano teacher in the Boston area was Frederika Tanzen Schildknecht, who gladly took little Magda as her pupil, and who said she might indeed be another Mozart. At the age of eight Magda Lanz performed with the Boston Pops Orchestra, sharing the stage and applause with two other prodigies, Akkoda Akiri and Marissa Lotspiech, of whom nothing more would be heard. Berman would say of his mother, there in Northampton: "Like ninety-nine point ninety-nine percent of great artists of every sort since the dawn of history, my dear mother, Magda, fell victim to audience shortages and a talent glut."

He said of talent in general: "Beware of gods bearing gifts."

So, although Magda Lanz continued to practice piano for three hours every day, until botched shock treatments following the birth of a comedian zapped her memory and aplomb to flinders, she set out to become a physician. She attended Knightsbridge's superb public schools and then drove daily in her own Mercedes convertible to and from Boston University, where she studied premedicine. A plain woman, and somewhat dumpy, albeit coming and going in a $60,000 form of transportation, she fell in love with a pretty-faced, redheaded, baritone, predental student: Bob "Paddy" Berman. As luck would have it, this "paragon of manly schmaltz," as his own son would come to call him, was also a former Junior Golf Champion of Barnstable

County, Cape Cod, where his folks lived. His dad owned a shoe store in Hyannis. It isn't there anymore. And did Magda's duffer father and her sandtrap Romeo ever hit it off!

Bob and Magda were given a $45,000 wedding at the Knightsbridge Golf and Country Club, and then the shit hit the fan big time! Magda found herself pregnant, and the rest is history. Berman: "Imagine how my father felt, only twenty-two, in his first year of dental school. How would *you* feel if you stuck your dingdong into a woman, with the best of intentions, and she exploded?" Or, conversely, one might wish to ask: "How would you like it if, through no fault of your own, you were booby-trapped protoplasm? Or her son?"

Gil Berman on the subject of his birth, which ruined the lives of both his parents: "When the doctor dangled me upside down and spanked my butt to start my breathing, I didn't cry. I said, 'A funny thing happened on the way down the birth canal. A bum came up to me and said he hadn't had a bite for two days. So I bit him.'"

After the booby trap went off, Magda and Bob Berman, one has to say, both behaved honorably and resourcefully within the strict existential limits Fate had set for them. As luck would have it, those limits, according to Berman, were "more like inner tubes stretched between fence posts than like barbed-wire such as once ringed Auschwitz and Alcatraz, because they had plenty of money. Money is dehydrated mercy. If you have plenty of it, you just add tears, and people come out of the woodwork to comfort you."

Yes, and each of his parents made the most of such momentum

as he or she had been maintaining before, and again, shit hit the fan. His mother continued to play the piano for hours every day, and she took up making artistic scrapbooks of current events, and she was a queen bee in a hive of doctor and lawyer bees, and nurse and hairdresser bees, and a nanny bee and then a tutor-and-companion bee for her child, and on and on. And there was already a gymnasium in the basement, and an aerobics instructor bee to make her and her child stay in shape. One odd rule she made—and she got a lot of what she asked for—was that although her son could sit next to her on the piano bench while she played—she liked that—he was never ever to touch the keys. If he reached for the keyboard when he was very little, she would grab his wrist and say, "No, no, no, Gilly-willy. Gilly-willy be very unhappy if he touch the keys. Gilly-willy-woo cry and cry all night like Mama." That sort of thing, as though the Steinway grand were, in Berman's words, "a red-hot, potbellied, cast-iron stove in a hick-town hardware store."

Also, if he made any friends in the outside world, he wasn't to bring them home with him. A former kindergarten teacher would recall him as having been "a rather unusual child." She was unable to be more specific than that. She was eighty years old.

It is Gil Berman who is responsible for the analogy above: a childhood home like a beehive. It must have surely occurred to his dad as well. "Anyone preparing for a career in the healing arts," he said, "is bound to have heard about the lives of social insects at some point in his or her education, as the case may be. I don't see how Dad could not have thought of Mother as a queen bee surrounded by workers. So fucking obvious! That would make him a drone. As a drone he had done all a drone was supposed to do, which was knock up the queen. But he was not a bee, and so he stayed in dental school at Boston University, to which he had just been admitted. What else was he supposed to do?

"He asked his gaga wife if he could borrow her Mercedes to drive to and from BU, since she was never going to drive again, and there were four other cars. She said, 'You'll have to ask my lawyer.' So he did. The lawyer said he could. That was the last time he asked his wife for anything. If there was something he really needed, like money for gas or lunch, he asked her lawyer."

He asked the lawyer, "How about tuition? Should my parents keep paying that? They will if they have to." Berman: "He was just a kid, you realize, only twenty-three years old when the excrement hit the air-conditioning. He felt he had done terrible damage with his dingdong, and he had had zero opportunity to establish himself as head or even co-head of a biological family. At least Bob Berman could become an orthodontist instead of sitting around the beehive with his thumb up his ass. Could he actually ask for money?"

Bob Berman's strikingly specific boyhood dream of becoming an orthodontist formed on a golf course when he was only a caddy, had been about money, and lots of time for golf, and being a doctor, but a kind of doctor whose patients weren't sick, who could never up and croak on him. But in defending his career choice against funsters since the eighth grade, Gil Berman's dad had become, in Gil Berman's words, "operatically arioso on the subject of how important smiles were, and what meticulous planning and patience and surgical skills it took to fix one." A professor of his at BU Dental likened orthodontics to "civil engineering in a teacup." Gil Berman's dad loved hearing that. It was the truth.

Gill Berman: "The only proof my dad needed of the existence of God was a birdie or an overbite. And after he bought another man's practice in Boston with Mom's money, he started chasing women with his own money. Why not? He was warm and beautiful. He came back to the Knightsbridge apiary maybe once a month. I'd sit next to Mom on the piano bench while she hammered out a thunderstorm. Or I'd watch TV. I didn't have a clue as to who or what he was. Neither did Mom."

Dr. Robert Berman, DDS, did in fact attempt to relate to his biological son when the son was a sophomore at Knightsbridge High. He took him for a ride in what had been the boy's mother's convertible Mercedes, "so they could talk." That's right! You got it! Dr. Berman was still driving what had become a priceless antique, not because he was cheap but because the car was glamorous. Gil Berman would say of that trip that he himself might as well have been the machine, and the Mercedes the fascinating personality, since his father talked to the car all the time. "The car had lost a lot of its pickup," said the comedian. "So when we were stopped at a stoplight with other cars around, Dr. Berman would say to the old Mercedes something like, 'Listen, old girl, in a moment that light is going to turn green, and nice people on important errands behind us will expect us as good citizens to jump ahead with all possible alacrity. Can you possibly do it this one last time? That's my baby.'"

When in Barnstable High School on the Cape, Dr. Berman had had what almost none of his classmates had, unless they had some kind of business to inherit: a blueprint for a future he could surely build—orthodontics. Others who played golf as well as he did, or could sing as well, might easily ruin their lives in sports or entertainment, where even more gifted people would surely cut them new assholes, would make them feel like something the cat drug in. That wasn't going to happen to young Bob Berman, and it didn't.

Gil Berman on his dad: "He was staunch! He held his course through all kinds of weather until he could at last drop anchor in the tranquil marina of orthodontics, where every patient has deep pockets, and no one dies." There in the Calvin Theater on December 11, 2000, Gil Berman might have been his father when his father was a teenager: "Let us pray: Our Father, which art in Heaven: Lead us not into the temptation of outsize expectations."

Magda Lanz Berman, Gil Berman's mother, died of cancer on April 9, 2000, having been a widow for twenty-three years. She had been a wife for only about half that long. She had been smoking two packs of unfiltered Pall Mall cigarettes since she was twenty, but she didn't die of cancer of the lung. She died of the quickie: pancreas. She died three months before her son the comedian entered the Caldwell Institute for the second time. That's right! You got it! Gil Berman had committed himself to Caldwell once before.

He committed himself the first time "when," in his own words, "I was a preemie, a neonate." He was also a newlywed, twenty-four years old. While in Las Vegas, Nevada, for the first time in his life, as a warm-up act for Marie Osmond, he had married a topless dancer named "Wanda Lightfoot," if you can believe it, when they were both tiddley-poo on LSD. During the wedding ceremony, during which they had promised to have and to hold and so on, he at least had the presence of mind to whisper hoarsely to his bride, who had a terrific set of knockers, "No kids, no kids."

Berman: "The next thing I knew, the knockers and I were somehow in a suite at the Ritz Carlton in Boston, one of my dad's old stomping grounds with babes. Monkey see, monkey do. The knockers, who was chain-smoking weed, may have asked to meet my mother out in Knightsbridge. That seems possible. I mean, what the hell? I had by then sworn off LSD and was limiting my intake to a crystal-clear detox medicine called 'Absolut.'

"So she said she was pregnant, and was so happy because she had always wanted a little baby to cuddle and nurse and so on. 'No abortion.' If she said 'No abortion,' it stands to reason that at some point in time I might have recommended that identical surgical procedure. Sometimes time flies, sometimes it creeps. On that particular occasion, time chose to fly, and the next thing I knew I was in a jail cell, just like the ones in the movies, and they told me my wife was in Massachusetts General Hospital with several teeth missing and a broken jaw, but that the baby inside her was still O.K. In my baroque experience, it is only in jokes that there's both good news and bad news: 'There's good news and there's bad news. The bad news is such-and-such, but the good news is such-and-such.'"

None of the above has been part of a public performance. It is a transcript of Berman's recorded admissions interview sixteen years ago, again: the first time he committed himself to Caldwell. Had he and his psychiatric social worker wished to fill in gaps in the tale, they had only to read accounts in the *Boston Globe*. When three policemen and a reporter brought Berman down from his suite at the Ritz on a freight elevator, for example, he said over and over again, "I am not Lee Harvey Oswald, I am not Lee Harvey Oswald."

On his "perp walk" through the lobby to the street, he said to the many people who just happened to be there, people of all ages, mostly educated and well-to-do, "Completely atypical, folks, utterly out of character, one hundred percent anomalous. Keep calm, keep calm."

In his admissions interview he was able to recall at least the flavor of the perp walk: "I am captain of the unsinkable ship *Titanic*, which is sinking, and I want all the spoiled, ritzy motherfuckers aboard not to make things worse by going nuts."

In a long piece two days later, the *Globe* concluded that hitting anybody was for Gilbert Lanz Berman, from one of the most distinguished old families in Knightsbridge, indeed "uncharacteristic," "atypical," and "one hundred percent anomalous." Ms. Florence Pate Glass, an English teacher at Knightsbridge High, where Berman had been president of the National Honor Society, testified: "Gilbert never fought, or even considered fighting. If there was a confrontation, Gilbert always turned the other cheek, although he was as manly and strong as three-quarters of the boys here. In one essay he wrote for me, and he was one of the eight best students I ever had, he said a formula as earthshaking as Einstein's 'E equals MC square.' It was 'Forgive us our trespasses as we forgive those who trespass against us.' No more 'An eye for an eye, a tooth for a tooth.' No more revenge!"

The reporter asked Ms. Glass, since the business about forgiving trespasses was in the New Testament, if Berman had shown an interest in Christianity while in high school. "On a sub-zero Christmas day in Hell," she said. "But I remember Gilbert asked me one time, 'Ms. Glass, if what Jesus said was good, why should anybody care a rat's ass whether he was God or not?'"

Ms. Glass said: "One thing really puzzles me though, along with beating up that poor woman, of course, is that he is now a comedian. I saw him on the *Tonight Show* two weeks ago, and I couldn't believe how funny he was. He used to be the most serious boy in Knightsbridge, too serious, I thought. I wanted to say to him, 'Gilbert Lanz Berman, can't you put down the world and all its troubles for at least ten minutes? It'll still be there when you pick it up again.'"

Ms. Glass asked the reporter what drugs Berman had been taking when he beat up his wife and was told it was alcohol and nothing else, and she said, "Sometimes all it takes is two martinis to transmogrify Dr. Jekyll into Mr. Hyde."

CHAPTER 2

Berman's Knightsbridge biology teacher, Dr. Aaron Edelman, termed him "an ardent Schweitzerite, a fully committed reverence-for-lifer." Edelman said, "It could be said of Gilbert as literally as it could have been said of his hero, Dr. Albert Schweitzer: 'He wouldn't hurt a fly.' I remember one time in the lab a cockroach ran across the floor, and a student named Cynthia Gottlieb stepped on it. And Gilbert said to her in that rich voice of his, 'Cynthia, I can't tell you how much I wish you hadn't done that.'"

A possible "extenuating circumstance," according to the *Globe*: "His father, the prominent Boston orthodontist Dr. Robert Berman, also runner-up two years in a row in the Wianno Pro-Am Tournament on Cape Cod, 1968 and 1969, committed suicide four years ago."

The denouement? Wanda Lightfoot through her lawyers asked for and received in absentia an uncontested divorce, a flat $1 million settlement, no alimony, no child support, and an order of protection against her ex-husband. That last was purely symbolic, since she had already left the state with the baby still inside her, and was having her name legally changed so that Berman could never find her. Berman in the year 2000: "That was back when a million was a lot of money. Nowadays you couldn't buy a cross-eyed shortstop for a season in the basement with the Seattle Mariners for twice that much."

In the year 1978 a reporter happened to spot Gil Berman at Logan Airport as Berman, in obedience to a court order, was about to leave for Milwaukee, Wisconsin, where a bus from the Caldwell Institute would meet him. He asked Berman what it felt like to give away a million dollars. And Gil Berman said this, appearing terribly weary and humbled, and not acting funny at all, according to the reporter: "*Tabula rasa*, friend. I feel like shit but my slate is clean."

Dr. Robert Berman, DDS, committed suicide in the autumn of 1977 at the age of forty-two, his son Gilbert's age there onstage at the Calvin Theater in the year 2000. Dr. Berman, DDS, did the big trick by means of carbon monoxide while sitting in his BMW convertible, with his seatbelt fastened and the top down in a closed garage on Cape Cod. The garage belonged to Mrs. Arnold Kirschenberg, a young and recent widow, a former girlfriend from Barnstable High School who, like Dr. Berman, had married a lot of money. She lived next door to the waterfront estate of the Kennedys in Hyannis Port, where the murdered brothers John Fitzgerald Kennedy and Robert Francis Kennedy had learned to swim and sail.

His son, Gilbert, was then nineteen, a freshman at Columbia. He had a daughter he didn't even know he had, not that she could have made any difference, telling him how much she loved him, begging him not to do it and so on, that sort of thing. She was only three years old then. And she wouldn't find out her biological father was a long-dead Boston orthodontist until, at the age of twenty-five, she tracked down her still unmarried biological mother, Mary Kathleen McCarthy, who worked as a receptionist for a veterinarian in Fresno, California, and who told her about him. So there was no biological father to whom she might introduce herself with all possible modesty. She did find out, at least, whence came her red hair. Mary Kathleen McCarthy's hair was brown. The name of the daughter, who was put up for adoption at the age of three months, was Kimberley Berlin.

Here's the story: Mary Kathleen McCarthy, an orphan, a Roman Catholic, had worked as a receptionist for Bob Berman in Boston for three years. She knew he was married and was devoted to his wife, although she did nothing but play the piano and make scrapbooks of items in the *Boston Globe*, and made no sense when she was talking, and they had a son who was at the top of his class in high school. But she could not help herself: She fell in love with him. He was indeed lovable, "a paragon of manly schmaltz," as his son would call him: good looking and sexy, but overwhelmingly considerate, and sentimental about the human race in general, quick to reward, forgive or comfort, or boost a loser's self-esteem. He was a people person if there ever was one.

Even after Gil Berman's dad fucked Mary Kathleen McCarthy on her desk after hours, in a moment of passion, *her* passion, with the telephone ringing and ringing, and knocked her up when she was twenty-four, she was still able to say to the redheaded Kimberley Berlin in Fresno: "Your father was a people person if there ever was one. He never took his eye off the sparrow. If you couldn't get along with Dr. Berman, you couldn't get along with anyone. And he could be so funny. Laugh, I thought I'd die."

And Mary Kathleen was surely not the first woman in history to find a man so lovable that she would have died for him, if that would help. More common, and more in practical harmony with the apparent intentions of evolution, one would think, have been women who died for children, children as children, not necessarily their own. The sacrifice Mary Kathleen performed for Bob Berman was a near-death experience for her, since she would never see him again. But it required only that she not tell him she was carrying his child, and that she quit her job and head for the other seacoast, where she would have that child and put her up for adoption.

When Gil Berman said celibacy was like not lighting a cigarette, he had no idea that this might have some bearing on his father's life. But it might be said that it was Mary Kathleen's match that lit the cigarette of Dr. Berman. And she knew that. She took full blame for what became Kimberley Berlin. She made the time-honored blunder of deciding a man should know how much he was loved, even though they both knew there was nothing either one of them could do about it: sort of like in an opera. What such women seldom realize, if they've never done it before, is that such an operatic confession in real life will cause their own bodies and souls to insist on copulation. She confessed, then cried.

He put his arms around her and said, "There, there," and off they went to the races.

Gil Berman was asked by a psychiatric social-worker during his first stay at Caldwell why, in his opinion, his father killed himself, although his father was in good physical health and was only forty-two. His father left no note, unless fastening his seatbelt first was some sort of note. He had given no indication to his hostess that, as soon as she was asleep, he was going to kill himself. And Berman said this: "I dunno. Don't ask. I hardly knew him. He came home to Knightsbridge less and less, and I don't blame him. When he did come home, he had to look at Mother's latest scrapbooks and say how much he liked them. And then she would play and play the piano, and I would sit on the bench next to her, so he would have to yell if he had anything to say to me.

"The fault was mine, not his. I'm afraid I treated him as an invader, an intruder. I told him I hated golf, and my teeth were coming in nice and straight. I was very close to my mother because I was so sorry for her. Now see the corner you've backed me into? What do I say next? That my father killed himself because his own son could not like him? Thanks a bunch. This much I know: I never heard him mention the Holocaust."

Yes, and on the CD *Who's Sorry Now?* Berman posits this conundrum: "Who's kidding whom? We're having a War on Drugs? The biggest American industry in dollar volume, number of employees, and persons and even nations directly or indirectly affected by it, is the thwarting or bankrolling, manufacture, shipping, and sales, wholesale and retail, of mind-bending, mood-enhancing, or blackout chemicals, including alcohol. Half the banks and brokerages in California and Florida would go bust if it weren't for invested profits from the drug trade. But don't worry: The War on Drugs might as well be a war on glaciers, with the soldiers armed with ice picks and smoking joints."

And then he intoned: "Let us pray: 'Our Father which art in heaven, Congress shall make no law respecting an establishment of religion, or prohibiting the free exercise thereof; or abridging the freedom of speech, or of the press, or the right of the people peaceably to assemble, and to petition the Government for a redress of grievances. Amen.'"

And then he called the President of the United States "a corksocker."

And then he said, "Nobody wants to admit it, for obvious reasons, I guess, but the swastika wasn't a pagan symbol. The Germans weren't pagans. They were Christians, and the swastika was just one more version of a Christian cross, like the Maltese Cross, the Celtic Cross, the Cross of Lorraine, the Red Cross Cross, Saint Andrew's Cross. Hitler's party was the National Socialist Party, and the swastika was a working man's cross made of tools, of axes. Only kidding, folks."

A male kid in the audience there at Northampton shouted this to Berman in the year 2000: "Hey Gilbert, who's gonna win the War on Drugs?" It was a keen and jagged question, for everyone there knew Berman was now a recovering abuser of or experimenter with a veritable *smorgasbord* of shit, except for booze, by no means all of it illegal. Quite a bit of it had actually been prescribed for him.

Berman's reply would make it onto TV and in the papers the

next day. There were reporters but not TV cameras there. "The War on Drugs," he said, "is one hell of a lot better than no drugs at all." Irony! His message, missed by the papers and TV, because one had to be in the theater to hear how he said it: He sure missed drugs, and he was now terrified, as he should have been all along, by their puissance and ubiquity.

The line wasn't original with Berman, either, which, again, he would have admitted, if timing had not been of the essence. He had come across it in a book about the "Roaring Twenties," the Prohibition Era, when thousands upon thousands of heavily armed law-enforcement people, at least half of them half in the bag, were mobilized in order to make people stop drinking alcohol, not even wine or beer. Can you *believe* it? This really happened! And according to the book, a humorist named Kin Hubbard said in print back then: "Prohibition is sure a lot better than no liquor at all."

It was at Columbia that Berman's life became, among other things, of course, a sequence of mind-bending substances, usually taken in moderation, and on the advice of friends who had tried them. The belief that one could thus fine-tune one's wits or charm or place in the universe thereby was particularly reputable at Columbia, because several of the psychopharmacological artists calling themselves "Beatniks" had come from there. One, Allen Ginsberg, had written such good poems while a confessed drug-user that he had been elected to the American Academy of Arts and Letters! As for alcohol, which Berman was still drinking back then, Eugene O'Neill, Sinclair Lewis, Ernest Hemingway, and John Steinbeck, not Columbia grads, to be sure, but

American winners of Nobel Prizes for Literature, were all certifiable alcoholics.

And the greatest of all mental-health theorists, Sigmund fucking Freud, was on cocaine.

The night that Berman, still an amateur comedian, premiered his routine about the impossibility of teaching evolution or anything else in a New York City ghetto public school, he first swallowed six two-milligram tablets of a patented amphetamine whose trade name was *Ritalin*, whose street name was *speed*. The pills had been prescribed by a doctor for his roommate Barry Dresdener, who, still taking them, would go on to become rich beyond the dreams of avarice as a vice president of Microsoft.

Moments before Berman strode up to the microphone at Cutty Sark, he chased those "six little darlings," as he called them, with two shots of brandy from the bar.

The mistress of ceremonies introduced him, then asked him, on mike, "How you feelin' tonight?"

"Blitzkrieg!" he said.

She topped him. She said, *"Gesundheit!"*

Yes, and after being discharged from Caldwell for the second time, Gil Berman made up several jokes about sobriety. He called it "the drug of choice for kindergarten through the first six grades." He said, "Sobriety is ten times more hallucinogenic than LSD or angel dust. If you haven't taken a trip on sobriety, or as they call it on the street, 'cold turkey,' you ain't seen nothing yet." And he was so curious about what sobriety was doing to him that it might have been a famous drug he hadn't tried yet, like "roofies," say, the so-called "date-rape drug."

He had a joke about roofies: "Lips that touch roofies will never touch mine." He compared his detoxed self with what he had been when he made *Who's Sorry Now?* That CD's opening lines were these: "Listen: If there was ever a man who should never have been a husband, that's me. If there was ever a man who should never have been a father, that's me. If there was ever a man who should never have even been alive, that's the booze-hound and coke-head who's here tonight to sell you on the many delights of de-destruction."

That pre–Taj Mahal Gil Berman ranted on from there, inter-rupting himself again and again with guffaws of agony, to tell of the violence that had ended his first and only marriage and that had caused him to be jailed and separated from his then-pregnant wife for what he thought would be forever. He did not mention on the CD that the wife he slugged in the jaw was gravid, or that he'd wanted her to get an abortion. But he did say how pitiful she looked after he knocked her down. And sober Berman found himself now wondering, as so many critics had when the disc was released, how anyone could find that part of it funny.

When he recorded it, and was on snorted speed, he had thought himself hilarious. He now wondered if the CD's popu-larity, in any case limited to persons his own age and younger, hadn't been engendered by morbid fascination with such a grotesque act of self-crucifixion.

No such yowling atonement, or even a mild admission of guilt of any sort, had so far been part of what had come pouring out of him since his second discharge from Caldwell, the stuff he was now trying out before a live audience for the fifth time there in

Northampton. It seemed to Gil Berman that drug-free Gil Berman was much more at peace with himself, as though he had settled whatever problem or problems had made him so desperate in *Who's Sorry Now?* He was familiar, as are all graduates of Caldwell, with this adage: that the problem in the life of an alcoholic is alcohol, and that the problem in the life of a drug abuser is drugs. Up to now, Berman had found this truism more of value to therapists than to patients. It gave therapists the simplest specifications for what they could call a cure. But Gil Berman, watching drug-free Gil Berman like a hawk, found him unimpaired as a wit and scourge of every sort of institutional stupidity and hypocrisy that was murdering not just common decency, but the planet itself.

What was lost? Self-pity. Another poignant line not original with Gil Berman: "Good riddance of bad rubbish."

You bet! And drug-free Gil Berman was still saying, in one way or another, because it had to be said, what in *Who's Sorry Now?* had provoked such pro forma outrage on the part of what he called "militant ostriches fighting the War on Drugs." He was still saying that drugs, over-the-counter, prescribed, or against the law, were as pervasive in modern America as cars or TVs—"or, for that matter, Kleenex and toilet paper"—and as potentially beneficial. Drug-free Gil Berman was still saying that the government, instead of fighting "Keystone Cops battles" against popular drugs outlawed at random, should be teaching Americans about all of them and admit that most, but certainly not all, if used in moderation, could be "sort of life-enhancing, like Kleenex or toilet paper."

From *Who's Sorry Now?*: "Please join me in my war on Bayer Aspirin and Phillips' Milk of Magnesia. Call out the Eighty-second Airborne! Aspirin makes the lining of my stomach bleed, and milk of magnesia makes me shit my brains out. And the only reason I'm not at war with General Motors is that state and local governments make sure people know how to drive a fucking Pontiac Trans-Am. Otherwise, I'd say let's do to Detroit what we did to North Vietnam with such satisfying results, which is bomb it back to the Stone Age."

Much of what Gil Berman tried out in Northampton in 2000 would be part of his CD *If God Were Alive Today*, put on sale in April of the year 2003. A few of those bits, all by themselves, including the one about artificial intelligences gossiping to each other about human beings, would be played at his memorial service at The Players, his club in New York City, in November of that year.

Cause of death? Morphine overdose, self-administered for permanent relief from the pain of the same cancer that had killed his mother. His age? Exactly forty-five to the day. Berman died in his business suit and basketball shoes, with a note pinned to his regimental-stripe tie. His regiment? The Coldstream Guards. His note? It was an epitaph he recommended for himself: "He lasted three years longer in that fucking Chinese fire drill than his dad did."

He was indeed given that epitaph, which made history as the first instance, in modern times at least, of the word "fucking" being incised into a headstone. Gil Berman, one last time, in his farewell note: "Symbols for fucking are nowhere to be found in the Pyramids, the Dead Sea Scrolls, the Elgin Marbles, or on the Rosetta Stone."

CHAPTER 3

Quoting yet again from what Berman said in Northampton when he had three more years to endure: "Political correctness has made many old-time, ethnocentric, shamelessly racist Caucasian metaphors and similes as offensive as 'shit,' 'fuck,' and 'asshole,' say, would be if yelled in church. Our Constitution, after all, the Law of our Land, after all, for which sailors, soldiers, marines, and coastguardspersons are paid to die, says implicitly, although, I must point out, not explicitly, that persons of color are people. So be it. I can take a hint."

Berman paused, as though ready to take up another subject. But then, as though driven to risk all in the name of common sense and justice, let the chips fall where they may, and said: "Listen. I say to the nonwhites in this audience tonight, and you know who you are: 'Please, must American eloquence be so emasculated that no one, no matter what color, and I include yellows, can no longer use that most sublime metaphor for confusion and hysteria in stressful situations, which is 'Chinese fire drill'? If the firepersons don't get their balls in an uproar about that expression, why should Chinks?

"Listen, I will make a deal with all yellows here tonight, and may their gods give them all good things: I will give up 'Chinese jibe,' if I can still keep 'Chinese fire drill.' Sailors here, and again I don't care two pins what race they are, know a Chinese jibe is when you are sailing before the wind in a sloop, without a care in the world, and all of a sudden the wind wraps the sail around the mast like a World War I puttee. I swear on my mother's grave that I will never again say 'Chinese jibe,' if only I can keep on screaming, whenever there is a monster fuckup on the order of this presidential election, 'Chinese fire drill!'"

Again, this was the night of December 11, 2000, and the voting for the president of a nation of one-quarter billion, whether George W. Bush or Albert Gore, had been so FUBAR, so fucked-up beyond all recognition, that the justices of the United States Supreme Court were now holding a new election in private just among themselves. Berman: "I don't know why we haven't let nine political appointees choose our presidents all along. No chance for a tie! And I must say I am honored that you came to hear me tonight, rather than staying home and watching the electronic tantrums on your erasers. I call TVs 'erasers' because they have not only wiped away the entire human experience to date, but whatever it was they were wetting their pants about only fifteen minutes earlier."

The last time Gil Berman himself had voted in any sort of election was when he ran against Cynthia Gottlieb for the presidency of their junior class at Knightsbridge High. Cynthia Gottlieb won, and she would eventually become, as Cynthia Gottlieb Schaffner, lieutenant governor of the State of Colorado, and then, even as Berman was performing at the Calvin, secretary of transportation under President George W. Bush. Bush, although the Supreme Court hadn't yet elected him president, was already naming members of his Cabinet. People cynical about politics were already calling Cynthia Gottlieb Schaffner "a twofer": both a woman and a Jew.

Berman said he visited Northampton's public library that afternoon, wanting to find out about Lord Jeffrey Amherst, in whose honor a nearby college and town were named. "Turns out this local hero made the world safe for democracy," he said, "by giving the chiefs of hostile Native American tribes blankets from the beds of Whiteskins who had smallpox."

He really had gone to the library that afternoon. He had discovered that the silence of a library, somehow always on the verge of uproar, could mute the twang of his need for drugs, provided he had a mission there. On his way from his hotel to the library, though, to find out who Lord Amherst was, he noticed that he was being followed by a large woman who, in his own words, "looked like a driver of an eighteen-wheeler on the turnpike from Hell to Pittsburgh." He was used to being sneakily tailed by plainclothes cops who, he supposed, were hoping to get fifteen minutes of fame by jailing a celebrity. Nor had such stalkers been invariably disappointed. Before his disorderly conduct at Trump's Taj Mahal, they had caught him smoking a joint backstage in Toledo, Ohio; snorting powdered Ritalin, or "speed," in a bus

station men's room in Corpus Christi, Texas; and in deep conversation with a fifteen-year-old prostitute who looked twenty in
Saint Augustine, Florida. He had not wanted to fuck her. He
thought she might know where he could buy cocaine.

But as for the woman stalking him in Northampton, he had
to ask himself: "What kind of cockamamie police department
outside Nazi Germany would have duties for a Diesel-dyke that
monumental?"

He thought he had ditched her by going in the front door of
an art gallery, out the back, and into a parking lot that the gallery
shared with the Nellie Prior Academy on the hill behind. But ten
minutes after he got to the library, in she barged. She didn't get
anything to read, but sat down at a table twenty feet away from
him, and stared everywhere but at him, and drummed nervously
on the tabletop with her fingertips until somebody told her to
stop it.

Here's what that was all about: This person was Martha
Jones, a deinstitutionalized lunatic sixty years old, turned loose
with pills in Ithaca, New York, where she had relatives she could
stay with. She had seen Berman perform there the week before,
onstage at Ithaca College. She followed him to Northampton
because she believed that the greatest prophets had preached
goodness as stand-up comedians, only pretending to be unseri-
ous. She was convinced that after Jesus was through preaching
"Blessed are the poor in spirit: for theirs is the Kingdom of
Heaven," and "Blessed are they that mourn: for they shall be
comforted," and "Blessed are the meek: for they shall inherit the
earth," and "Blessed are they which do hunger and thirst after

righteousness: for they shall be filled," and so on, he winked and said, "Only kidding, folks."

And now she thought Gil Berman was a reincarnation of that joking Christ.

And there she was, front row center at the Calvin Theater, looking up at him with goo-goo eyes. He spoke directly to her. "I don't deserve to look this good," he said. This was compassionate. He was thinking how awful it must be to have to go through life so unattractive. She was a gerontomorph, with grossly exaggerated facial features usually taken to connote maturity. In a word: Martha Jones was a female Neanderthal.

But Gil Berman's apology for his own paedomorphic good looks would in any case have been the segue into his next bit, which was about automobiles, to wit: "I read in the paper the other day," he said, "about the death of what was believed to have been the oldest living thing in New England. It was a mulberry tree on Cape Cod, in Barnstable. It wasn't a New World native like those to whom Jeffrey Amherst made the gift of smallpox. No. Its mama and papa trees had to have been in merry England, home of capital punishment for property crimes and the Magna Carta. When they counted the rings in its trunk, there were 283 of the motherfuckers! Just think: If that tree had had wonderful ears and a brain like lucky us, it might have heard people talking about everything from the French and Indian War, in which Lord Amherst so distinguished himself, to the War on Drugs, in which no one and everyone is a winner." He paused, pretending to ransack his own brain for something else to say.

And then he said, "That tree, when a sapling, must have

crossed the Atlantic on a sailing ship. Imagine crossing the North Atlantic, whether on an errand for good or for evil, with only the restless winds of the planet to get you where you next wanted to do your thing. How's that for science fiction? And now we have automobiles, powered by the most addictive and destructive drug yet discovered, which is gasoline. Yes, and in one eensy-weensy century we have sucked the last drop of petroleum from our planet's sweet flowing breast. For what? For an orgy of transportation whoopee, friends and neighbors. For shame! You think around-the-clock fucking and sucking is bad? Listen: The farts of our internal combustion engines have wrecked the atmosphere as a protective shield, and as anything a mother would want her child to breathe. You think people farts are bad? The polar ice caps are melting, I shit you not. The last polar bear, the last King of the Arctic, died ten days ago, and a mulberry stump on Cape Cod will soon be under three feet of saltwater.

"And I ask you again, friends and neighbors: 'How's that for science fiction?'

"There's bad news and there's good news," he said. "Martians have landed in New York City. The good news is they only eat homeless people, and they pee gasoline. Only kidding, folks. Actually, a team of anthropologists from Mars has been studying the American way of life for the past ten years. They went back home last week on account of global warming. They didn't want to be roasted or drowned. But their leader said before lift-off that there were two things about Americans no Martian could ever understand. 'What is it,' he said, 'about blowjobs and golf?'"

He cleared his throat and pretended to make sure his voice

was still working. He did this by singing scales as he used to do in singing class at Knightsbridge High: "*Do, re, mi, mi, mi,*" and so on. Again: What a voice! Jesus Christ!

And then he said, "I know you ladies from Smith College here tonight are ardent feminists, flat heels and no makeup, preparing to beat men at their own games in the marketplace. But you know what I think?" he asked with apparently profound, baritone concern. "I think this is a national tragedy. Honest to God, and this kidder is not kidding this time: I think educating a woman is like pouring honey into a fine Swiss watch. Everything stops."

He was rewarded with an incredulous, collective gasp from the audience. It went up in the theater, as he would later declare, "like a great big purple hot-air balloon." He was on a roll with political incorrectness, and he didn't stop. "You want to know what I think about the Chinese fire drill about men and women that's been going on for a million years now? Try this on for size: All women are psychotic and all men are jerks."

The audience was lobotomized.

He laughed at them. "Boy, did I ever goose you. You're the goosiest bunch I've spoken to since B'nai B'rith. But let me restore your dignity with a therapeutic technique I perfected while lying on my back on a craps table in the Trump Taj Mahal." What was supposed to happen next, and had happened at the University of Vermont; and then at his alma mater, Columbia; and then at Boston University, where his mom and dad met; and then Ithaca College, where Martha Jones had fallen in love with him, was this: He would coax the audience into standing up and clucking like hens who had just laid eggs.

He was a hypnotist.

Gil Berman said, "And that's the end of my show, folks. You're such polite people, you're probably ready to clap your hands, whether you liked the show or not. Over the past thousand years, at least, nice people like you have been clapping for poor sons-of-bitches or daughters-of-bitches onstage, whether they really liked them or not. Slapping your palms with your palms can mean anything. It's high time we came up with a new form of applause that is optional, and that can mean only one thing: 'Really loved your show, no shit, no shit.' How about clucking like hens who've just laid eggs, not that I've laid eggs tonight. At least I hope not."

Silence.

"Applaud, please. I stand before you, having completely drained myself in order to make you happier to be alive than you were before, but you sit there like statues made of apple pan dowdy."

Silence. Sheepishness.

As he had done four times before, Berman came to the apron of the stage, wiggling his fingers at the audience like a mesmerist, and intoned droningly: "You are hypnotized. You have no will of your own. You have just laid eggs. Now stand up and cluck, cluck, cluck. Show how proud you are."

Silence. What had happened at all four previous shows would surely have happened again. One person would have clucked, and then another. And then, in about three minutes, everyone, with a few exceptions, of course, would have been standing and clucking louder and louder, and laughing like crazy when he or she wasn't clucking, and flapping his or her folded arms like chicken wings, and loving himself or herself in a hilarious demonstration of therapeutic mass hysteria.

And Berman would have vanished.

But Martha Jones had seen his act in Ithaca, and to her the slowness of the audience there to respond to commands by this avatar of Jesus was an abomination. She wasn't going to allow that to happen again. She had shuddered and swayed to her feet. She now faced the audience and belted out these words in the voice of the toughest truck driver on the turnpike from Hell to Pittsburgh, and only capital letters will do:

"DO WHAT HE SAYS! THIS MAN IS NONE OTHER THAN JESUS CHRIST!"

Everybody thought the thug in a muumuu was part of the act!

Berman was rooted to the stage like a mulberry stump in Barnstable.

What were members of the audience to extrapolate from this situation? They were being tested, they thought. The next move was up to them. What were their alternatives? Any sudden and stentorian announcement about Jesus would have left them momentarily thunderstruck. But now they could evaluate the source: an obvious clown, a man dressed like a woman, and part of the show. So far as they knew, Gil Berman was still completely in charge. So if they did not feel at all like laughing, which they didn't, that was because he did not want them to laugh. Did he really think he was Jesus? Anyone crazy enough to believe that about himself or herself, as the case might be, would still not have been so crazy as to pay a clown, of all symbols, to announce the fact. Nor had Berman at any point in the evening seemed in the least fire-eyed or messianistic.

Silence.

Berman, who couldn't really have been catatonic, was up there onstage pretending to be catatonic, or so they thought. He wasn't about to tell them what to do next. They should be able to figure that out for themselves, if they were such a smart bunch of college kids. Applaud with their hands? He had mocked doing that for its quite possible insincerity. Cluck like chickens? Please!

And then they got it, or thought they did: This enemy of hypocrisy up there on stage wanted no hypocrisy from them, should any part of his show have disappointed them. And he was demonstrating that he was as austere about praise as he was about sex. He didn't need it, didn't want it. Let others be obsessed by praise.

In character!

What to do? They did it. They departed the Calvin Theater as quietly as ghosts.

Holy shit! What a sacred moment.

In a few minutes, the silence broken only by the sounds of shuffling footsteps, the opening and closing of doors to the outside, and the clangor of a passing fire engine, there were only four human beings still inside the Calvin. There was Berman onstage. There was Martha Jones, who had subsided back into her seat, as Berman would later say, "like a mountain of apple pan dowdy." Her Neanderthal features were now a tabula rasa. There was a rosy, roly-poly, uniformed Northampton policeman who had been on duty backstage.

And loping down the aisle from the lobby came Sheldon Hayes, the very tall, very thin, white-haired, sixty-year-old theater manager, who, years ago, had left nearby Florence, Massachusetts, for New York City, in the outsize expectation of becoming a Broadway actor. His long white hair was tied in back with a blue velvet ribbon in a ponytail. He was thrilled and incredulous. Sheldon Hayes believed he had witnessed a theatrical masterpiece.

Sheldon Hayes stopped first before Martha Jones, front row center, and he said, "You were terrific! I damn near excreted a piece of masonry!" And he wheeled so quickly, in order to look up at Berman, who was now teetering on the apron of the stage, that he could not see that Berman's stooge, supposedly, might actually be a corpse now.

And Sheldon Hayes called Martha Jones a "he." He said to Gil Berman. "Where the heck did you find him? He was marvelous! He told me he was part of the show, and had to be front row center, but I couldn't imagine how you were going to use him. You are a genius. That's all I can say. How in heck did you know it was going to work that well? And you know what people whispered to me as they were leaving? They were saying things like, 'Cool, cool,' and 'Super cool.' One kid said, 'I'm just going to have to go back to the dorm and think about this. No TV tonight.' They were all so reverent. The Jesus Christ business shocked them, made them so reverent, made them think about all *kinds of* stuff all at once, which is what the greatest teachers do. But what a crazy risk you took with the Jesus thing. Talk about a chance for a big-time backfire. But you son of a bitch, you got away with it.

It worked, it worked. Crazy like a fox. They're all going to go home and think now."

Sheldon Hayes wasn't gay. Like Berman, he was a neuter. Later that evening, Berman would describe him as "an albino giraffe."

Gil Berman for the moment accepted what had happened. What else could he do? What else should he have done? But then he took a good look at Martha Jones, although he did not know that was her name, or even whether she was a man or a woman. And then he said to the albino giraffe, "I think maybe you'd better call an ambulance." And the roly-poly, rosy police-man, whom Berman would later call "a sentimental hippopota-mus," and who was standing next to him now, was already talking to police headquarters, two blocks away, on his cellphone, on his own having decided that Berman's "stooge" really might be dead.

He thought he had big news, but headquarters had even big-ger news for him, which Berman and Sheldon Hayes could hear in the shushing overflow from the instrument's earpiece. This person was a woman. Her name was Martha Jones. She was a deinstitutionalized mental patient who had stopped taking her pills and run away from her brother-in-law's house in Ithaca, where she was living; that she often looked dead but really wasn't; and that her niece Lily Matthews was there at the station right now, ready to drive her aunt back to Ithaca. The cops in Ithaca, as soon as Martha Jones was reported missing but not dangerous, had learned at the bus station there that the unmistakable Martha Jones had bought a bus ticket from Ithaca to Northampton, which would require her to change buses at Syracuse, and then at Springfield. But damn if she hadn't made it!

The sentimental hippopotamus clicked off his cellphone, and he said to Sheldon Hayes and Gil Berman, as though they hadn't heard any of it, and with all possible clinical gravitas: "It's a she. She only looks dead. We don't have to do anything. She hasn't been taking her pills. Her niece will be here in a minute to pick her up."

Here is additional clinical information about Martha Jones that might have been interesting, but surely not useful at that point in time, as the three men stood around in the Calvin with their thumbs up their asses, so to speak, waiting for the niece to arrive: Martha Jones had been born with ambiguous sexual organs and glands and musculature. These things happen. Several such persons had elected to compete as female athletes with great success. Martha Jones had elected to overeat and go nuts in muumuus instead.

CHAPTER 4

The following is a transcript of a recording of what Gilbert Lanz Berman said to a psychiatrist five years his junior, post–Taj Mahal, during his second stay at Caldwell, after he had been there a week. This was the first of two sessions. He would fire her after the second one. She was Dr. Helen Newman Klein, whose office was in nearby Milwaukee. She would come to Caldwell, which had no resident psychiatrist, but only internists and dieticians and psychopharmacologists and aerobics instructors and psychiatric social workers and the like, at the request of patients, like Berman, who wanted and could afford to pay for seriously probing talk therapy that might deal with life problems beyond mere substance abuse. Dr. Klein was an absolute knockout—great body, great smile.

After Berman fired her, she would opine that Berman, rich as Croesus, had summoned a psychiatrist so he could tease her for his own amusement and cajole her into prescribing a sleeping pill, Desamol, that they wouldn't give him at Caldwell.

She said to a Milwaukee colleague, Dr. Walter Streit, who was on his way out to Caldwell to take over Berman's case, "I hope your pockets are full of Desamol, and you know what the fundamental illness of stand-up comedians is." Dr. Streit said he didn't know but that he hoped to find out, and she said, "Ingratitude."

So here we go, with "B" for Berman and "K" for Klein:

K: How do you do, Mr. Berman? I'm Dr. Klein.

B: Do have a seat, Doc. Take a load off your feet. I keep thinking today is Tuesday.

K: Today is Tuesday.

B: That's what I keep thinking. You know why cream is so much more expensive than milk?

K: So much more butterfat?

B: It's because the cows hate to squat on those little cartons. You bring me my Desamol like a good girl? I have a lot of trouble sleeping.

K: You have to ask your doctor out here. You've been here once before?

B: Who squealed? O.K., you got me. And the last time I was here, they sent me home to Mother with a bushel of Desamol, so I could sleep.

K: Times change. Side effects and lawsuits announce themselves. Prescriptions change. Desamol isn't recommended for men anymore, except for sex offenders.

B: Actually, there's nothing wrong with me this time, thank goodness. I'm back at dear old Caldwell University for my class reunion.

K: Which class is that?

B: Upper. What other class can afford to stay here? But as long as you've come all the way from Milwaukee, maybe you can give me some advice about my brother Heathcliffe.

K: A brother? I looked at your files here this morning.

B: Oy! The Gestapo!

K: No mention of a brother.

B: Black sheep! Heathie can't hold a job. Had a swell job in a panty-girdle factory. He was pulling down ten thousand a year! Got canned. So I bought him a one-way ticket to Switzerland.

K: Where Heathie punched holes in cheese.

B: Much too obvious, Doc.

K: Shot in the dark.

B: They had him clean birdshit out of cuckoo clocks. Too much responsibility for brother Heathcliffe. So I pulled some wires, Doc, called in some markers, used my connections with certain unnamed persons in the White House, and got him a position hammering corks into bottles in a winery. Lasted three lousy weeks, Dr. Strangelove. His co-bottlers at Manischewitz said my brother was nothing but a mean and stupid corksocker.

K: Tell me about his love life.

B: None of your beeswax, Ms. Nancy Drew. Want to talk about mine?

K: What is there to say? Throughout history, celibacy has been a respected, even revered predicament, if we can call it that, in which some of our greatest thinkers have found themselves, long before you started taking Desamol.

B: For sleep.

K: And the exact opposite of Viagra.

B: Oysters aren't the great aphrodisiacs they're cracked up to be.

K: Heck!

B: Ate twelve of 'em one time.

K: Oh?

B: Only three of 'em worked.

K: Must have been before you came here the first time. And that must have been after your father died.

B: Too obvious, Doc. My dad committed suicide in an old girlfriend's garage, so that explains everything? Listen, in one of Plato's dialogues, a formerly great cocksman is asked what it's like not to be a great cocksman anymore, and he says it's like being allowed to dismount from a wild horse.

K: Not all horses buck.

B: Are you making a pass at me?

K: I was thinking of horses. Now that you mention it, though, women must be making passes at you all the time.

B: Shows how little you know about women. They don't make passes at gay men, do they? And I've taught them that a neuter is another sort of man they don't have to attract with a lot of silly horseshit like butts and boobs, and that's such a relief to them. They can think for a change. They can wear shoes that feel good. They can be genuinely friendly with other women instead of being on their guard against them. Ever notice how free women are to really like each other a lot when they're shopping or having lunch or going to the theater with a gay guy? Same thing with a neuter, and we'll soon be coming out of the closet by the millions, thanks to me. No AIDS, no babies, no marriage, no breech births, no postpartum depression, no orders of protection and broken jaws, no divorce. Women, make passes at the flaming neuter Gil Berman? Why spoil a good thing?

K: So, you have many women friends.

B: I have many people friends. In the words of Thomas Jefferson: "We the people." And next time, either bring Desamol or don't wear perfume.

K: I'm not wearing perfume.

B: Somebody is.

K: When you were taking Desamol, why weren't you half-asleep all the time?

B: You take Ritalin.

K: Another side effect, I've read, is constipation.

B: You take Phillips' Milk of Magnesia, the old tried and true.

K: And headaches.

B: You take Excedrin or Anacin or Tylenol or Bayer Aspirin or Bufferin.

K: And occasional dizziness.

B: You sit down or hold onto a telephone pole or the nearest meter maid. And no lipstick next time.

K: I'll wipe it off right now.

B: You would look so pretty while you were doing it, that would just make things worse.

K: I think you're kidding me, Gil Berman.

B: Wouldn't you think something had gone terribly wrong if I didn't fall in love with you? Be honest.

K: The scrapbook.

B: What scrapbook is that? Mother made a million of them, to which I, the greatest of all comedians, as you may have noticed, have now fallen heir, along with an eight-bedroom house in Knightsbridge, two Steinway grand pianos, and Boston slum properties almost without number. It's in my file here that my mother made scrapbooks?

K: I didn't know that about your mother. I just found this one scrapbook in your file, and it seemed so odd: It had such an expensive cover, and the clippings were so neat. They were laid out on each page so artistically, almost as though by a professional layout artist.

B: She could have been a professional layout artist. I could have been a professional layout artist. You could have been a professional layout artist. You married? One of Mother's scrapbooks wound up out here? The only proof of the existence of God my mother needed was the morning paper, a pair of scissors and Elmer's Glue, and a piano. Jesus, I must have talked so much about her scrapbooks the first time I was here, somebody must have written her doctor to ask if they could please see one. But that doesn't seem very likely.

K: You didn't bring it with you? I thought maybe you were the one who made it.

B: What's it about? Barbra Streisand's fight with her hairdresser? The Cuban Missile Crisis? It was all so fucking pathetic. When Mother was a little girl she made scrapbooks about what a great pianist she was, the even greater one she would surely become. About three of 'em, now mine, all mine. She stopped when there was nothing more about her in the morning paper. But after she went bonkers, after the shock treatments, she started making them again, almost as though anything that happened was something for which she was somehow responsible and should be proud. And she was proud! She didn't even know who Dad was anymore, just that he was this sweet young man who came by from time to time because he loved to look at her scrapbooks. I wasn't all that clear either about who he was, and what the fuck he was doing there. He was a paragon of manly schmaltz who loved scrapbooks and thought it was great how nice and straight my teeth are. Which they are. Don't tell me you haven't noticed how straight and gleaming white they are. Don't lie. You have delivered yourself into the presence of the world's most dreaded shit-detector. So God knows how and God knows why: One of my poor mother's scrapbooks made it all the way to a file cabinet in Salem, Wisconsin. What's it about? Elizabeth Taylor marries for the thirteenth time? Vietnam?

K: I thought you surely knew. Now I'm sorry I brought it up. It's about your nervous breakdown in Boston.

B: You're shitting me! She made a fucking scrapbook of that?

K: You were in the morning paper, not once but several times.

B: Oh, keeeeerap!

K: Since you only now found out about it, let's put off talking about it until the next time.

B: Keeeeeerap! Burn the motherfucker!

K: When you go home from here, where exactly is home?

B: Keeeeeerap!

K: Where is home?

B: Where is what?

K: Where is home?

B: Home, my dear Docky-wocky, docky-wocky-wicky-woo, is a condominium to die for in Manhattan, across from Gramercy Park South, to which I hold a key, and five doors down from the Players, a club for theater people in which I hold a membership, and where I find more congenial company than at which you can shake a stick. And six blocks west is a saintly physician who will prescribe anything I want, even if he never heard of it before, for he himself is on LSD.

K: And will there be someone waiting for you in your nice condominium?

B: Of course! You think I would yearn to be back there if there weren't a significant other waiting?

K: Another neuter?

B: You got it!

K: Can I ask who it is?

B: If you promise not to breathe his name to anyone.

K: Goes without saying.

B: Gilbert Lanz Berman. You would fall head-over-heels in love with him, if you could see his smile. You'd want to marry him.

K: And be labeled a home-wrecker? And I must be going now. And I am so happy you have plenty of Phillips' Milk of Magnesia.

B: Touché, dearest of all possible Helens. Touché, touché.

CHAPTER 5

The Calvin Theater there in Northampton is named in honor of Calvin Coolidge, the thirtieth president of the United States. He was born and raised nearby. When the American humorist Dorothy Parker was told in 1933 that Coolidge was dead, she said, "How can they tell?"

Yes, and catty-corner and across the street from the Calvin is the Hotel Northampton, where Gil Berman had hired a room for one night only. A car and driver from a limo service had brought him from Manhattan, and the driver had a room in the same hotel. The plan was that they would go to Knightsbridge the next morning, where Berman would try yet again to strike some sort of bargain with his childhood home. At least it was empty now, and it was his, all his. He could fucking well, in his own words, "put out a contract on it, call in the wreckers, if it still won't stop putting crazy messages in my head like the CIA."

Berman could easily afford such expensive transportation.

And he no more needed the fees he got for public appearances than his father had needed what he was paid for orthodontics. He and the driver, Don, had not become friends on the trip. Berman had not wanted to talk, but preferred to daydream, snooze, or simply take in the scenery. He was not one to befriend those who drove him. He said to one driver who tried to strike up a lively conversation, "Look, I'm trying to think back here. If I need a Sancho Panza, I'll let you know."

At the end of the trip that driver said, "Just one question, Mr. Berman, if it won't interrupt your chain of thought too much. Who the heck was Sancho Panza? A baseball star?"

After Martha Jones's niece got her aunt out of front row center in the Calvin and into the family Honda out front and headed for Ithaca, Berman returned to his hotel room on the third floor. He found himself phoning Dr. Walter Streit, the psychiatrist who had replaced Dr. Klein back in Wisconsin, back at Caldwell. During his drug years, he regularly called up this acquaintance or that one, twice his congressperson, without knowing why, and then waited to see what would come pouring out of him. In a *Rolling Stone* interview back then, he said: "To me a telephone is like a bung in a barrel, only I'm the barrel. When the person answers I just turn on the bung, and what comes out is almost always new material, wonderful stuff I've never heard before. I laugh like hell, and so does the guy on the other end."

Drug-free Berman hoped sobriety would still let him do this. He would soon find out.

Dr. Streit had given Berman his home phone number, saying,

"In case something has bothered you so much you don't know what to do next." Dr. Streit was already in bed, although it was only 8:30 in Wisconsin, which is on Central Standard Time. Dr. Streit was drunk as a hoot-owl, lying on his back with an open copy of "The Myth of Sisyphus" by Albert Camus for a roof over his face, when the phone on his bedside table rang and rang. He picked it up, and here's what he heard: "Doc, this is Gil Berman. I'm fine. Don't worry about me. But you can't believe what happened at my show tonight. What a fucking zoo! The theater manager looked like an albino giraffe. The cop on duty looked like a sentimental hippopotamus! And there was this deranged woman who looked like a gorilla in a haystack. And then this circus midget came in with another cop, who looked like a transsexual iguana! Honest to God! And the midget, a girl, said to the gorilla in a haystack, 'Aunt Martha, you've stopped taking your pills again. Now look at the trouble you've caused for these nice strangers.' And the gorilla in a haystack said, 'I just wanted to make sure this man knew that he, like the holy clowns Abbie Hoffman and Lenny Bruce, was a reincarnation of Jesus Christ.' All I need to know from you, Doc, is where do I go to get detoxed from sobriety?"

Berman paused for breath. He had been guffawing in agony, in the style of the opening lines of *Who's Sorry Now?* When he got set to spout some more, though, he realized that the phone was dead. Dr. Streit had apparently hung up on him, which was indeed the case. Some doctor!

"Sobriety," incidentally, is generally understood to mean a life without one specific mind-bender, which is alcohol. But get a load of this: Gil Berman had been entitled to credit himself with sobriety, when defined that narrowly, for eighteen years! He hadn't had an alcoholic beverage since his first stay at Junkie Junction, at the Caldwell Institute. When he spoke of sobriety there in Northampton, he meant he was at last free of the drugs that had, not only in his own opinion, but in the opinions of several colleagues and critics, as well, made him deeper and quicker as a comedian than he would have otherwise been.

On the subject of alcohol abuse, in fact, he had become quite the prude. When he was in the company of people who were drinking booze, he would order "a double Shirley Temple, please, and don't hold back on the grenadine." Grenadine is a cloyingly sweet, nonalcoholic, red-orange syrup flavored with pomegranates and is the most exciting ingredient in a Shirley Temple cocktail. A Shirley Temple cocktail, in turn, is what grownups who are drinking hard liquor, tossing down what the late W. C. Fields called "Nose Paint," order for any children they happen to have somehow brought with them into a drinking establishment.

In the beginning, immediately after Gil Berman got out of Crawford for the first time, persons serving him thought he was kidding, since no adult in history had ever ordered a Shirley Temple. So there was bargle-bargle before it was clear he was dead serious: "Where's the manager? I want to see the manager. I want a Shirley fucking Temple cocktail, and you, for reasons impossible for this sane citizen of the United fucking States of America to fathom, will not let me have one," and so on. That sort of thing.

In more recent times, though, his lusty consumption of

Shirley Temples had become as widely known as his chastity and wealth, to the point that he was often served a Shirley Temple without having ordered one. The sobriquet he had given Shirley Temples in performances and interviews, moreover, had become patois for many gin-mill professionals. The nickname was "Foot-in-the-door." A waitress might say to a bartender, "Two feet in the door," and the bartender might reply, "Two Shirley Temples coming up." Someone at the Hotel Northampton had been so hip as to have a pitcher of Shirley Temples and a bucket of ice waiting for Berman in his room.

In his *Rolling Stone* interview he declared: "Drugs are science. Alcohol is superstition."

A Gil Berman joke about Caldwell, which he gave gratis to a comedy team, since it took two people to make it work:

Al: You're looking so happy and healthy, Joe. Just get out of Junkie Junction?

Joe: Better than that, Al, I just shipped the wife and mother-in-law up to sunny Wisconsin for new pills, old religion, and detox.

Al: Found their stashes yet?

Joe: Nothing to it, Al. Hired a dog and handler from Rent-a-Narc.

Oh, sure, and Gil Berman, there in his room at the Hotel Northampton after being hung up on by a psychiatrist, felt like something the cat drug in. He wasn't funny anymore? He'd been funny enough at the Calvin. And the demented poor soul in the front row hadn't wrecked the show, but had accidentally created a theatrically effective, if confusing, coda.

So?

And then it came to him: He himself loathed what he had said to the doctor. Why? Because what had happened at the theater after the niece arrived had in fact been so noble, so spiritually dignified, so moving that Berman had almost wept. Why couldn't he have said so?

"Circus midget"? The niece, only eighteen, was indeed short, but not freakishly so: maybe five feet. Why not "teenage Virgin Mary"? Berman was so impressed with her that he called police headquarters afterward from his room to find out her full name and, if possible, her address. Her name was Lily Tracy Matthews.

The theater manager, Sheldon Hayes, was an "albino giraffe"? Really? And what about "the transsexual iguana" and "the sentimental hippopotamus"? Why not "three angels" instead?

And "the gorilla in a haystack"? Why not "a sacred mountain of faith and humility"? That is what she really was.

Primitive, patriotic, self-anointed critics had sent him hate letters in the past, saying, in effect, in one way or another: "You don't even need the money or women. What do you think you're doing, shitting on everything we hold dear?" Were they right that much of what he shat upon deserved to be honored as sacred? Here was what he had just shat upon on the telephone:

Into the Calvin came the short but shapely niece with a cop whose features were indeed, albeit through no fault of his own, sexually ambiguous and objectively reptilian. She had parked her dad's Honda Accord right outside. The iguana looked at the seeming corpse front row center and said, "Oh my God. Holy shit." But then he said to her: "Excuse me, Miss Matthews. I just didn't know what we were up against."

And she said: "I told you how important this person is to me, how much I love her."

He said: "No disrespect." He had been indoctrinated by her on the way over to this effect: that her aunt, no matter what she looked like, was actually majestic. And the rosy, roly-poly cop took his cue from him, and, like the iguana, positioned himself at an unthreatening distance from Martha Jones, but with arms outstretched, signaling muscular but gentle potential helpfulness.

Berman: "If CPR were required, they knew how to give it. Inside even the meanest uniformed policeperson there is a Florence Nightingale screaming to be let out."

Gil Berman and the tall, pony-tailed, white-haired theater manager, the failed actor Sheldon Hayes, clambered up onto the stage, lest there be violence. And Lily Tracy Matthews, the niece, said to the muumuued corpse: "Aunt Martha, you haven't been taking your pills again. Now look how much trouble you've caused these nice strangers."

Only the lips and tongue of the corpse moved. This time their words were high and teeny-weeny, like Minnie Mouse. They said: "I just wanted to make sure this man knew he was a reincarnation of Jesus, like Lenny Bruce and Abbie Hoffman." The mouth closed was lifeless as the rest of the body again. Martha Jones wasn't going anywhere, and there has to be the suspicion, as must be suspected of every mentally disadvantaged person, that inside lurks a master or mistress illusionist. Sane or not, Martha Jones had contrived to make an awfully nice young woman take complex and loving care of her.

Lily Matthews, who hadn't seen Berman's show in Ithaca, who never watched TV, and so had never seen him on a talk show, looked up at Berman and Sheldon and said, "Which one of you is the great comedian?"

"Guilty as charged," said Berman.

She said, "Please tell her you know you're Jesus Christ."

"I know," said Berman.

"It has to be the whole thing," she said. "You have to say the whole thing, or we'll spend the rest of our lives in here."

Before he could stop himself, Berman said, "It's time to call a forklift." The instant that slipped out he could have killed himself. Of all the heartless things to say! Who the *hell* did he think he was: Count Dracula?

Sheldon Hayes hissed at Berman with undiluted hatred. "Jesus Christ, man." It wasn't a cue. It was an expletive.

The two cops were now leaning backward, their arms dangling helplessly behind them, their faces aghast. How could they play this serious game with such a smart-ass making wisecracks? Lily Matthews had bared her clenched teeth and was sucking in air through the cracks in between them.

Gil Berman made a gesture that may have been instinctive for all comedians throughout history, comedians who have really stunk up a joint with abysmal tastelessness. He held up his hands palms outward, petting the hostile air as though it were an enormous sheepdog, meaning: "Hey, gimme a break. Gimme a chance, you guys. You guys know me," and so on.

And then he said directly to Martha Jones, squatting so his eyes were almost level with hers: "I admit it, Aunt Martha: I am Jesus Christ, I am Jesus Christ."

From Martha Jones's lips and tongue, still Minnie Mouse, came these six words: "You bet your ass you are." But she was still a corpse, not about to leave there. And the iguana said to Lily, "What do we do now?"

Before answering she sent darts of contempt from her eyes into those of the great comedian. Then she said, "First I have to sing to her. And then we all have to sing so we can march her out of here." Can you beat it? Martha Jones had made it all the way from Ithaca to Syracuse to Springfield to Northampton, and to the public library and then the Calvin Theater, in a town strange to her, without any songs or marching. Lily felt the need to explain: "After she completes a mission, she tries to die, hopes to die." Sheldon Hayes and the two cops nodded in perfect understanding.

Gilbert Lanz Berman didn't nod. He was too upset about the bad impression he had made on this perfect micro-woman. He had fallen in love with her. Without Desamol to protect him, he had fallen in love with Dr. Helen Newman Klein back at Caldwell as well. He had so far found love an easily manageable side effect of sobriety, just as he had managed the occasional dizziness caused by Desamol: no need for panic or drastic revisions of lifestyle. The feeling would pass. What eighteen years of daily doses of Phillips' Milk of Magnesia had done to his lifestyle was something else again. His large intestine had become slack and pouchy and demoralized, causing him to be a loner, if for no other reason than that at any moment he might become what he himself had called, in a high-society proctologist's office, "a carpet-bombing fart machine."

Now the perfect Lily knelt before her catatonic Aunt Martha and crooned to her, in perfect pitch, the song "Somewhere" by the late genius Leonard Bernstein, a chain-smoker of cigarettes like Gil Berman's mother, from the great musical comedy *West Side Story*. Yes, and having heard the song, Martha Jones was on her feet and simpering. Lazarus! But she did not appear to be ready to go anywhere. At any moment, she might just sit down again. Lily explained: "She feels safe in there. It's so cold and wet outside. But she loves parades. Is there some song we all know that we can sing while we march her out to the car?"

Sheldon Hayes jumped down from the stage, so excited to be taking part in a miracle. He said: "Row, Row, Row Your Boat!" He was back in nursery school! Asserting leadership, he broke into song, clumping his feet in a march tempo. The two cops and Lily joined in, singing the endless song while marching in place. Soon Martha Jones was singing and making the floor boom with her heavy footfalls. Talk about happy!

Up the aisle, through the lobby, and out under the marquee went the nursery-school pageant: IF GOD WERE ALIVE TODAY. And Gil Berman, still onstage in a vacant house, felt like the loneliest man in the universe, with nobody to understand him and take care of him. And then came farts in a veritable fusillade.

CHAPTER 6

In his hotel room there, having been hung up on by his Wisconsin psychiatrist, Gil Berman noticed that his telephone's message light was on, and had probably been aglow all the while. He called down to the front desk and found out a woman had left a sealed envelope for him.

Berman: "I hope it isn't a summons." Anything for a laugh.

"Looks like a Christmas card."

"Ravishingly beautiful woman?" Anything for a laugh.

"About thirty, I'd say. Red hair like yours."

"Long lost relative." Anything for a laugh.

He went down to get it, pretending his cupped hand was a cellphone as he crossed from the elevator to the front desk: "Look, you ugly schmuck, I'm going to have you killed, and your kids, too." Anything for a laugh.

He sat on the couch before the fireplace there in the lobby, a blaze of propane on hollow logs of iron. It felt good, and he thought of a line he might use at his next scheduled appearance, which would be at Connecticut Wesleyan. Something like this: "Here's a cheap high you Methodists might want to try: If it was good enough for John Wesley, it ought to be good enough for you: Bake your brains in front of a fireplace."

He would later say that, as he opened the envelope before the fire, he "felt like an English country squire in a Sherlock Holmes story, opening a curious envelope that had arrived in the post that day." It was indeed a Christmas card, and timely, since Christmas was only two weeks away. It was nondenominational, secular humanist, since the salutation, in gold cursive letters on its cover, was simply: "Joy." No exclamation point. The printed message inside could hardly have inflamed the most short-fused Zoroastrian or Baha'i or Parsi, or crustiest crackpot village atheist, for it was simply this: "May the season's warmth fill your home with happiness."

Beneath, however, was this handwritten personal message in blue ink: "Hi, funny man, I am your sister. I am currently an English teacher and drama coach and soccer coach and dorm mom at the Nellie Prior Academy, a private college preparatory school (har-dee-har-har) for girls here in Northampton. Here's my DNA, if you don't believe it. Where's yours?" And there was an arrow pointing down to a dot, which was red. Menstrual blood? He sure hoped not. The signature was "Kimberley Berlin."

He thought little more about it. Women did not make passes at him, but it was common for one to demonstrate that she thought technological progress was as much a crock of shit as he did. The red dot was evidently an attempt at satire on all the yahoo horseshit about genetic engineering: how cloning sheep and decoding the human gene chain and so on were going to make being alive so much more rewarding than it had been to date. "O.K.," he thought to himself. "So what else is new?" He put the card back into its envelope and sailed both into the blaze of propane.

But that wasn't quite the end of it. His brain, which he had come to consider a quite separate person, autopsied the event in search of a joke. It found one! Bingo! Pay dirt! Try this: "If DNA technology discovers who it is in the Tomb of the Unknown Soldier, will they kick him out?"

He mused that if this Kimberley Berlin had declared herself his daughter rather than his sister, and the desk clerk said she had red hair like his, it might have shocked him for a minute or two. He did have a daughter out in the world somewhere, who would be eighteen, too young to be a prep-school teacher. For that daughter's sake as well as his own, he had thought about her as little as possible. What good could he be for her, or *she* for him? He thought it fair to assume that Fate had given her a stable, loving, dependable stepfather. How would it help anybody if a biological father were suddenly to blindside her in the backfield, so to speak? He did nonetheless find himself reminded, there in front of the fire, of another sealed envelope handed to him by another woman when he was still in Caldwell for the second time.

The woman? Dr. Helen Newman Klein. From the transcript of their second and final session of talk therapy:

B: What's this? A fan letter or hate mail?

K: I thought you should read it at the start of this session. Then we can both make jokes for the rest of the hour. Why did the chicken cross the road, and so on.

B: Before I open it, I do want to tell you what I've learned from a fellow patient, a heroin addict who is also an ornithologist.

K: As long as he isn't your brother Heathcliffe.

B: I'll bring you up to date on Heathie in a minute. He's in Samoa.

K: I'm sure.

B: The ornithologist is Dr. Orville Schittbein, PhD, of the Colorado School of Mines. I took the opportunity of asking him what the white stuff was in bird poop. Haven't you always wondered that?

K: I've led a sheltered life. I'm still a virgin as far as bird poop is concerned.

B: You know what he told me? You're not going to believe this.

K: Time to open the envelope, Mr. Berman.

B: He swears the white stuff in bird poop is bird poop, too.

K: And the winner is? Pretend you are Heathcliffe, Mr. Berman, passing out Oscars at the Academy Awards, and open the envelope.

B: That's going to be so hard. We're so unlike, Heathcliffe and me. Heathcliffe and I. Sometimes I wonder if he isn't the love child of Babe Ruth and Elizabeth Barrett Browning.

But he did finally open the envelope, and here was the message she had put inside: "Aside from his many years now of abuse of cocaine, amphetamines, Desamol, and Phillips' Milk of Magnesia, the patient Gilbert Lanz Berman may be distressed by his inability to acknowledge and deal with the fact that twenty years ago, he, figuratively rather than literally, buried his wife and child alive."